GHOSTLY ORDEAL

A Harper Harlow Mystery Book Twelve

LILY HARPER HART

HarperHart Publications

One

As far as winters go, Southeastern Michigan was mired in a particularly brutal one. Whisper Cove, which was located on the water, was being inundated with lake effect snow at least two times a week. And, while Harper Harlow happened to love a pretty snowstorm as long as she could sit in front of the fireplace watching it, the season was starting to feel too long.

"I think there should be a rule," she said as she peered out the window with a mug of hot chocolate in her hand. "Snow is for Christmas and people who want to live in Canada. It should be banned from every other location once January kicks off."

Her fiancé Jared Monroe looked up from the couch, amusement lining his features. He had a catalog resting on his lap and adoration in his eyes. "You don't like being snowed in with me, huh?"

Harper, her blond hair longer than normal, shook her head. "It's fine. I don't mind being snowed in with you. It's just ... I kind of like it when we can spend our quality time together outside."

"You mean you wish we could hammock." Jared's gaze traveled back to the catalog. "I was just looking at hammocks. Why don't you come over here and join me so we can pick one out, huh?"

Harper merely rolled her eyes. "I'm not going over there. I know what will happen if we snuggle together on the couch and look at hammocks. We'll end up ... you know."

Her expression was so dainty, so out of place, Jared could do nothing but laugh. "Since when are you opposed to doing ... *you know?*" His eyes gleamed with flirty intent.

"I'm not opposed to it. I just think you have to wait until after five."

He furrowed his brow. "Since when is that the rule? We've done it ... *you know* ... plenty of times before five."

"Yes," she agreeably bobbed her head. "But all those times were in the morning, before noon. We didn't technically get up from bed before doing it so they were considered continuations of the previous evening, which is totally allowed."

Jared was beyond confused. "I didn't realize there were rules we had to follow."

"Not necessarily rules," she hedged. "It's just ... it's weird to do it in the middle of the afternoon."

Jared moved the catalog to the coffee table and fixed his full attention on her. Their new house — which was directly across the road from her old house — was almost completely put together. They still had several boxes hidden in the front closet so they could ignore them without guilt and were now looking forward to adding new pieces ... because there were currently some big holes in their decorating schematic.

The plan was to spend the day — they both had it off — filling some of those holes. Apparently Harper had other things on her mind.

"I have to believe I've romanced you in the afternoon before," Jared pressed. "It seems completely unlike me to ignore that time of day."

"You have romanced me in the afternoon," she agreed, sipping her hot cocoa and grinning. She'd picked up on the change in his mood and found it entertaining. "It's only been at appropriate times, though, like when we were on vacation that one time ... or we had the day off on a weekend."

She said it with such conviction that Jared found himself wondering if she was right. "You've been keeping track, have you?"

"It's not that I've been keeping track as much as I would've noticed if we played Hide and Seek in the middle of the afternoon. I'm weird that way."

"You're definitely weird," he agreed. "You're just the right amount of weird, though." He pursed his lips as he regarded her. "I don't suppose you'd like to break that streak, would you?"

She chuckled, obviously amused. "I don't think that's a good idea. It's the middle of the day, after all."

"A snowy day." He jabbed his finger toward the window by way of proof. "I think we should have a serious discussion about this. I don't want to be predictable."

"We're not predictable." Harper finished her hot cocoa and left the mug on the dining room table before cutting over to the couch where Jared sat. "I see ghosts for a living," she reminded him. "You believe me without question and never give me grief about it. How could that ever be construed as predictable?"

It was a sound argument, but Jared was having none of it. "Why don't you sit on my lap when you say that?"

"No way." Her expression was playful as she darted around his outstretched arms. "We have a million things to do. We're supposed to be deciding on furniture and other necessities. We have one couch, a really old table my mother found at a garage sale and insisted we borrow from her, and like two pots and pans. We need to get serious about decorating this place."

"Oh, I'm serious." His eyes sparked with interest as she did a little dance. "Let's take the catalogs into the bedroom and flip through them in there."

"If we go in the bedroom ... ."

"We'll have a lovely afternoon," he finished. "You'd better start running now because I'm going to catch you, Heart."

She chuckled. "I don't think we should be inappropriate like this. We should be grown-ups."

"Start running." His voice was barely a whisper. "I'm going to catch you."

"I believe you've already caught me." She edged toward the hallway. "Are you going to do it twice?"

"I'm going to do it for the rest of our lives." He hopped to his feet. "Here I come."

AN HOUR LATER, JARED HAD A lazy smile on his face as Harper cuddled next to him in bed. The snow continued to fall outside, creating a cozy atmosphere as he tucked in the blankets around her.

"So much for your theory regarding afternoon entertainment," he drawled.

She giggled as she brushed her hand over his chest. "I haven't been proven wrong on that point. We're supposed to be picking furniture. That was the whole point of taking the day off together."

"I thought the whole point was that we saw the forecast over the weekend and didn't want to deal with the snow," he challenged. "We decided to take personal days ahead of time so we could watch the snow fall from the safety of our new house. We even stocked up on groceries and everything."

"That was simply an added benefit."

He moved his hands over her back, taking a moment to enjoy the way her body fit against his. "We should look at furniture, though." He blindly felt along the small table he was using as a nightstand and came back with a Pier One catalog. "Oh, look what I found."

Harper laughed as she rolled to his side, remaining comfortable in the crook of his arm as he opened the catalog. "That's convenient."

"It is," he agreed, his hand automatically smoothing her mussed hair. "We have a lot of decisions to make, Heart. It's time to get serious." He used his most authoritative voice. "We have like five pieces of furniture and the only comfortable piece is the couch I brought ... and you hate the pattern."

She balked. "I don't hate the pattern," she countered. "It's just ... okay, I hate the pattern. I simply don't like red plaid. It's weird."

"So, we'll pick out a new couch."

He said it in such an easy manner that Harper felt odd arguing with him. Still, she knew it was necessary before they disappeared down a rabbit hole and found themselves in financial trouble. "We both spent a decent amount of money on this place," she noted, choosing her words carefully. "We have some put away, but I'm not sure it's a good idea to spend all of it on furniture."

Jared slid her a sidelong look. "What do you mean? You want to keep living like this? The only good pieces of furniture we have are your bed from the other house and the beanbag I brought from my teenage room at home."

"And the nightstand." She gestured toward her side of the bed, to where the matching nightstand rested.

"And the nightstand," he agreed. "We need another nightstand, though. I have stuff I like to keep close to the bed. Your dresser also matches the set, but it's not big enough for two sets of clothes, so we need another dresser."

"I got the set at Art Van. We can head over there."

Jared pursed his lips. "We will. I just think we should wait until it's not snowing. Maybe we can do that over the weekend."

"You just want to see if you can get in another round of naughty afternoon sex," she admonished.

"Is that a bad thing?"

"I guess not." She rested her head on his chest as he flipped through the catalog. "I wasn't trying to be a pain when I suggested we not spend all our money right away. It's just ... it makes me nervous to drain my savings account completely. When I first went into the ghost hunting business, I told myself that it would only be an option as long as I didn't go into debt.

"My parents screamed up and down about debt during their fights when I was a kid," she continued. "My father saw nothing wrong with debt and my mother absolutely hated it. She also hated not having nice things ... so she added to the debt as much as him. I mistakenly thought they were fighting only about the debt for a time, so it warped my view a bit."

"I guess that makes sense." He brushed his lips over her forehead as he considered what she was saying. "I don't see how we can add living room furniture without replacing the couch. It all needs to match."

"It definitely needs to match," she agreed. "That doesn't mean we need a new couch, though. The couch itself is comfortable. What if we just get a cover for it?"

"I didn't even think about that." His fingers were light as they trailed down her spine. "I don't see why we can't do that. Then we can get some comfortable chairs and a table. That table we're using looks as if it came from the world's worst garage sale."

"It probably did," Harper said. "My mother picked up a lot of dinnerware – and that table – from friends right before we moved. I'm guessing those friends couldn't unload the things we were given and that's how we ended up with them."

"That makes me feel better." He kissed her cheek and turned another page. "I get what you're saying about not emptying our accounts. The house was a big purchase. My job is regular, though. I'm not in danger of anything bad happening. I can take care of both of us going forward if it's necessary."

Instead of reacting with relief, as he expected, Harper fixed him with a dark look. "Excuse me?"

Jared sensed he'd stepped into the thick of it but wasn't sure how he managed it. "Um ... what?"

Harper's frustration was palpable. "I'm fully capable of adding to the joint finances."

"I didn't say you weren't."

"You insinuated it."

"I most certainly did not," Jared shot back, refusing to back down. "I know you're going to add to the finances. I never doubted that for a second. There's no need to get all worked up about it."

"What makes you think I'm worked up?"

"I've met you."

Harper's expression darkened. "I think you're being a pain in the butt. All I said was that I was capable of adding to the finances. We're doing this together. That's what we agreed on when we decided to move in together."

"And then we got engaged." He tapped the engagement ring he'd bought her with the help and guidance of her best friend Zander. "Things are slightly different now that we're getting married."

"How do you figure that?"

"Well ... for starters, you're going to be my wife."

Harper pulled back so she could prop herself on an elbow and stare at him. "And you're going to be my husband. How does that change anything?"

"It's my job to make sure you're taken care of." Jared barreled forward, oblivious to the minefield he was about to walk into. "I have to make sure you get everything you need and that's what I intend to do."

Harper narrowed her sea-blue eyes until they were nothing more than glittery slits. "And what's my job?"

"What do you mean?"

"If your job is to take care of me — probably because I'm a weak female, right? — then what's my job?"

It was only then that Jared realized he'd made a colossal mistake. "Oh, well ... ."

Harper waited, practically daring him to add to the trouble he was already facing.

"You're looking at this the wrong way." Jared regrouped quickly and squeezed her waist under the covers. "I wasn't saying that I didn't think you could help. I know you can help. I want you to help."

"You just think you have a greater responsibility to take care of me than I have to take care of you."

"No. That's not what I was saying." Jared extended a warning finger. He sensed the conversation slipping away from him and that's the last thing he wanted. "We're both equals in this relationship. You know I see you that way. Don't make this a thing."

"Oh, I would never make this a thing." Harper rolled her eyes as her phone dinged on the nightstand. "I think you've made this a thing all on your own."

Jared couldn't disagree with her, even though he really wanted to. "Ignore whoever that is ... especially if it's Zander. I thought we decided to spend the day together with no interruptions."

"Trust me. An interruption can only do you some good right now." Harper flopped on her side of the bed and answered the call. She expected to hear Zander on the other end. They used to share the house across the road together, and the proximity of the new house was one of the major selling points when Jared selected it because he knew Harper wouldn't do well if she was separated from her best friend, and they were still adjusting to not being on top of each other all the time. Instead of her best friend, though, she found her mother waiting with breathy anticipation.

"Hello, Harper." She sounded chirpier than usual, something Harper wasn't sure how to gauge.

"Hello, Mom." Harper ignored the face Jared made. Her mother was difficult under the best of circumstances. This was obviously not going to be one of those days. Still, she was glad for a break from the conversation. She sensed it would get out of hand before either of them could rein it in. "What's up?"

"Oh, well, you know." Gloria Harlow was the prim sort. She liked to get the niceties of a conversation out of the way before drilling deep. Harper was used to it so she didn't think twice when Gloria started to babble. "This snow is something, huh?"

"Yeah. I'm not a big fan of the snow," Harper agreed, wiggling away from Jared when he tried walking his fingers over her midriff.

"You're not out chasing ghosts in this, are you?" Gloria wasn't a fan of Harper's chosen profession. When her only daughter admitted to seeing ghosts as a child, she was convinced Harper was plagued with mental illness. It was only after a few harrowing rescues and other feats that shouldn't have been possible that Gloria began believing Harper was special. That didn't make her happy, however. In fact, there were times Harper was convinced her mother would've preferred it if she really was suffering from some form of mental malaise because that would've given Gloria something to fix.

As it was now, there was nothing technically wrong with Harper. That didn't mean Gloria wasn't regularly searching for a cure.

"I'm home," Harper replied, making a face when Jared's hand started creeping toward her. "Hold on a minute." She held the phone away from her mouth and glared at her fiancé. "I'm not happy with you right now. Stop doing that."

"Not until you forgive me." Jared tickled her ribs. "I don't want this to ruin our day."

"Oh, don't worry. I can tell from my mother's tone that she's about to tell me something that will ruin our day. You're free and clear from the blame." Harper returned the phone to her ear. "We're looking at furniture catalogs."

"Oh, that sounds nice." Gloria was obviously distracted because she didn't utter one passive aggressive comment when Harper brought up her furniture situation. Gloria had been fretting about the hodgepodge of furniture for weeks. "Do you think you can abandon that for a little bit and visit me?"

Harper found the question odd given the fact that her mother was a weather alarmist under normal circumstances. "Um ... well ... it's kind of bad out."

"It is," Gloria agreed. "I still need to see you."

"Why?" Harper was instantly suspicious. "Did you do something? If you vandalized Dad's property again I'm going to tell Mel the truth if he questions me." Since her parents were mired in the world's longest — and most bitter — divorce, Harper's mind actually jumped to what she considered the worst possible scenario. Her mother had been increasingly bold when it came to messing with her father.

"This has nothing to do with your father." Gloria was firm. "It has to do with me."

"Is something wrong with you?"

"Well ... ."

Harper's heart sank. "Are you sick?"

Jared, who was in the middle of trying to tickle his fiancée again, stopped playing and turned serious. Harper and her mother weren't especially close, but the illness of a parent was always a concern. "What's wrong?" he asked.

Harper shrugged instead of answering. "Mom, you need to tell me what's going on. I can't help unless you tell me the truth."

"Yes, well ... ." Gloria made a throat-clearing sound on the other end of the phone. "The thing is, I'm at Carl's house. You remember Carl, right? What am I saying? Of course you do. We've been dating for a few weeks now."

Carl Gibbons. That was his name and about the only thing Harper remembered about him ... other than he combed his hair in a ridiculous way to cover his bald spot. He was a divorce attorney, which is how her mother met him. She never dated her own divorce attorneys, but she was more than happy to erase a business relationship right from the start so she would be free to see whomever she wanted.

"I remember him." As far as Gloria's dates went, Carl bothered Harper less than most ... although that wasn't saying much. "Why are you calling if you're with your friend?"

"Because he's dead ... and I'm pretty sure he was murdered."

Whatever she was expecting, that wasn't it. Harper's heart plummeted. "Are you serious?"

"Yes. I need your help."

She needed more than help, Harper surmised. She glanced at Jared, who obviously couldn't hear Gloria's end of the conversation and was still operating under the assumption that something was wrong with her physically.

"Give us a few minutes, Mom," Harper said finally, resigned. "Jared is with me. We'll be right there."

"Oh, thank you so much."

"We're going to need an address."

Two

"I don't understand." Jared dutifully climbed into jeans and a T-shirt without complaint, grabbing a comfortable flannel shirt from the closet and shrugging into it as he watched Harper mull over two sweaters. "Why would your mother call us instead of 911 if her boyfriend is dead?"

Harper shot him a withering look. "I would think that's rather obvious," she said. "You're a cop."

"I am," he agreed. "It's just ... how does she even know he's dead? Maybe he's unconscious and needs an ambulance."

"We'll find out soon enough." Harper settled on a black sweater and tugged it over her head, the ends of her hair standing on end thanks to the buildup of static electricity. "Do I look okay?"

Jared pinned her with a dubious look. "As compared to what?" he challenged. "Your mother isn't going to critique your outfit at the scene of her boyfriend's death."

Harper wasn't so sure about that. "You never know." She finger-combed her hair as she strode through the house and collected her boots at the front door. "Come on. I think she's freaking out."

Jared was directly behind her and didn't need urging. "I'm right here." He looked her over with a studied gaze, making his mind up on the spot. "Maybe you should stay here and let me check on her, huh? I promise I'll call the minute I know something."

"Don't even." Harper's cheeks flushed with annoyance. "I know you think I need to be taken care of, but I'm perfectly capable of handling my own mother. That's not going to change."

"And here we go," Jared muttered. "I don't want to fight. I didn't mean that the way it sounded. Most women would be happy to have a man who stands by them no matter what. I guess you're not most women, though."

"Are you just figuring that out?"

Harper shot him a look before grabbing her coat from the closet. "Let's go. I promised her we wouldn't be more than a few minutes."

"I'm coming." His earlier mood a distant memory, Jared slipped into his coat and grabbed his keys from the small console table that rested against the foyer wall. "We're going to talk about this later, though."

"I'm looking forward to it."

THE DRIVE TO CARL GIBBONS'S house took ten minutes despite the fact that it was less than a mile away. The roads were atrocious, and even though Jared had four-wheel-drive, he found himself struggling to make it through intersections because the plow trucks hadn't yet been through the side roads.

"This is a mess," he muttered as he navigated a particularly high drift. "I don't think anyone should be out in this."

"My mother needs help." Harper's tone was shrill, her knuckles white as she gripped the door handle and stared out the passenger side window. "She wouldn't have called unless she was desperate. She only calls to nag or when something is really bad."

And that, Jared realized, was the true crux of the problem. Harper was a barking mess because she couldn't wrap her head around her mother's fear. Jared knew Gloria on a cursory level — the woman was always pleasant to him and mentioned over and over that she was glad he'd found Harper so her daughter didn't have to spend the rest of her life alone — but he wasn't all that familiar with the woman's moods.

Harper was careful to make sure they didn't cross paths too often. Jared was convinced that was for his benefit because Gloria was obviously a difficult woman to deal with.

"It's going to be okay, Harper." Jared's voice was low and soothing as he pulled onto the correct street. "Whatever is happening ... I'm sure it can be easily explained. Heck, maybe he's not even dead." He chose to look on the bright side of things despite their circumstances. "It's possible your mother didn't get close enough to check. You know how she feels about icky things."

Despite herself, Harper let out a low laugh. "That's true. Maybe he's just sleeping very deeply."

"There you go." Jared wanted to reach out and capture her hand, show her some reassurance, but the roads were too treacherous to risk it. "What do you know about this guy? I can't remember if I've met him or not."

"You have." Harper made a face. "He was the one we went to dinner with a few weeks ago, the one at the steakhouse."

"Ah, the one who told us that steak made men more virile in bed." Jared smiled at the memory. "I believe we had fun imitating him later that night. I wanted you to dress up in a steak bikini and test his theory."

"Yes, I remember that, too." Even though she was agitated, Harper's lips curved. "I'm sorry for yelling at you earlier. It's just ... I'm used to people giving me grief about what I do. I tend to ignore it as much as possible, but it's not always easy."

"I understand that." Jared slowed his truck as he struggled to read the house numbers. "I don't believe I've ever said a thing about what you do, though. I mean ... I guess I did that first time I had you in for questioning. I was suspicious of you then, but it's not because I didn't trust you. I'd simply never heard of anyone really having your ability.

"I didn't doubt you very long," he continued. "I figured out you were telling the truth within days and I've always been on your side ever since that moment. Always. I'm going to stay on your side for the rest of our lives. That's why I asked you to marry me."

"And here I thought it was because of how cute I look in my fuzzy winter pajamas."

He snorted. "The fuzzy pajamas are only a bonus. As for the rest ... I know you're good at what you do. I don't doubt for a second you'll bring money into the household. That doesn't mean I can't help you occasionally, or you can't help me, for that matter. Once we're married, we're going to have joint accounts, right?"

"I guess." Harper was thoughtful as she tapped her bottom lip. "I still have to keep my business account with Zander. You know that, right?"

"I do. It's not an issue. I'm going to be your husband, Heart, not your lord and commander."

"Yeah." She looked more relaxed as he pulled into the driveway. "That's Mom's car." She leaned forward.

"It looks like she's been here a little bit." Jared glanced around. "There's already an inch of snow on her car."

"It's really coming down."

"Not that fast." Jared continued staring forward for a bit before killing the engine of his truck. "Come on. Try not to stomp around the house and leave snow anywhere — or touch anything — in case this really is something we need to worry about."

Harper nodded, grim. "Okay. Thanks for doing this."

"That's what I'm here for."

"I thought you were here for my afternoon delight."

"That, too."

GLORIA WAS A FLUTTERY MESS when she opened the door.

"I don't know what to do," she announced when the couple stepped into the entryway of the two-story abode. "I think he did this to make me crazy. There can be no other explanation."

"He did this?" Jared arched an eyebrow. "Are you saying he committed suicide?"

The look Gloria shot him was straight out of a how-to book on making your future mother-in-law hate you. "I have no idea. I'm not an expert on these things."

"Would he have committed suicide?" Harper asked.

"Oh, right." Gloria rolled her eyes so hard it was a miracle she didn't fall over. "I'm such a heinous hag to deal with he had to kill himself to get away. That's what you're saying, isn't it?"

"Not even remotely." Harper looked to Jared for help, uncertain. "I don't know what to do."

"Ignore her." Jared wasn't in the mood to deal with Gloria's brand of histrionics. "We need to focus on the problem at hand. Where is he, Gloria?"

Gloria extended a shaking finger toward a door on the right. "He's in there ... and it's not pretty."

Jared regarded her for an extended beat and then walked in that direction. He honestly wasn't sure what he would find on the other side of the door. Gloria was known for blowing things out of proportion. In her world, for example, a paper cut was the same thing as a bayonet wound. Still, what he found waiting for him in the living room was enough to make his blood run cold.

"Son of a ... ." He viciously swore under his breath as he stepped over the threshold, his mind going a million miles a second.

"What is it?" Harper asked, pressing close to his back so she could find an angle to peer around him. "Is he dead?"

"He's definitely dead." Jared swiveled and caught her wrists before she could sneak around him and taint the scene. "This also wasn't suicide." He was calm because of his job training, but he felt weary just thinking about the list of things he needed to check off. "I need you to do me a favor."

Harper stopped struggling to see the body and focused on him. She knew he wouldn't be asking unless something was really wrong. "What do you need?"

"I need you to force your mother to sit on that bench in the foyer and not touch a thing. It's important. You need to sit with her. I also need you to call Mel, tell him what's going on here, and ask him to get the medical examiner."

Harper had no trouble understanding that Jared was deadly serious ... which meant the scene on the other side of the couch was probably something out of a horror movie. "Okay. Um ... how did he die?"

"Badly."

"Jared ... ."

"I can't focus on that right now." He was firm. "I need to go by the book on this one. I'm sorry. Can you just do as I asked?"

She nodded without hesitation. "I'm sorry about this ruining our day. I'm sorry about the fight earlier, too."

"It wasn't really a fight." He meant it and kissed her forehead before digging in his pocket for a pair of rubber gloves. "You can't go wandering around the house. That's especially true for your mother. Can you please keep an eye on her? It could be very important before everything is said and done."

Realization dawned on Harper. "You don't think she did this, do you?"

"Of course not. I just need to make sure that we cover our bases. That means you need to help me."

"Okay." Harper knew better than to argue. Jared was in official mode now. That meant he was focused on his job. "I'll call Mel first thing. Hopefully he will be able to get here despite the roads."

"Faster is better," Jared agreed. "I'll be in here. Just ... don't wander around. Promise me."

"I promise."

MEL KELSEY WAS A MASS OF exaggerated growls and annoyance when Harper let him in through the front door.

"This had better be good," he announced, his cheeks a rosy shade of red. "My cruiser got stuck about three blocks down and the county road crews are going to have to get it out. I already placed a call."

"Oh, no." Harper felt horrible for him. In addition to being Jared's partner, he was also Zander's uncle. She'd known Mel since she was a small child and was quite tight with him. "That's terrible. I'm sorry."

"Yeah, well ... what are you going to do?" Mel removed his gloves and slipped them into the pocket of his coat. "Where is Jared?"

Harper pointed toward the living room. "I don't think it's good. He's being really quiet."

"Which means it's definitely not good," Mel agreed, his eyes briefly traveling to Gloria. "And why is your mother here?"

"She was dating the guy," Harper replied. "He's a divorce attorney. She came over to visit and found him."

"I see." Mel was growing increasingly uncomfortable with the situation as the facts came to light. "Well, I'll go in and talk with Jared and then we'll take it from there. The medical examiner is coming, but he's going to be way behind me. He's still at least thirty minutes out. Can you keep an eye out for him?"

Harper bobbed her head. "I'm on it."

"Thank you." Mel kept his smile in place as he entered the living room, but it evaporated quickly when he caught sight of the body on the floor. "Holy ... ."

"Yeah." Jared rolled his neck until it cracked. "It's ugly."

"He's obviously been stabbed," Mel observed as he circled the body. "I'm guessing a good four or five times."

"Yeah. There's too much blood to get a good number," Jared agreed. "We're going to need the medical examiner to determine that."

"Still, we're talking a great deal of rage here." Mel was fixated on the dead man. "His eyes are open, which means he was alive during the attack."

"Definitely," Jared agreed. "Given the way the blood is congealed, I'm going to guess he's been dead about twelve hours or so. Maybe a little longer."

Mel did the math in his head. "Then we're talking after midnight."

"I'm thinking probably about two in the morning, but we obviously need that confirmed."

"Obviously," Mel echoed, making a tsking sound with his tongue. "What do we know about this guy? I mean ... I think I've seen him around a time or two, but I don't believe he's a fixture in the community. At least he doesn't hang around the same places I do."

"Carl Gibbons." Jared was matter-of-fact. "He's a divorce lawyer who just happens to be dating Gloria. I don't believe she used him for her divorce, but we'll have to check and make sure. I know she's careful about not dating the guy who is currently handling her case."

"The case that will never end," Mel muttered. "I swear, she and Phil have been divorcing each other for what feels like forever."

"I'm guessing Harper would agree with that assessment."

"Speaking of Harper ... ." Mel darted a look in the direction of the door to make sure nobody was listening before continuing. "You realize that Gloria is going to be a suspect in this simply because she was dating the man, right?"

Jared was uncomfortable with the question. "I don't *know* that. I mean ... can you imagine Gloria doing this?"

Mel answered without hesitation. "Yes."

"You can?" Jared was taken aback. "But ... no way. She doesn't like getting dirty."

"That doesn't mean she didn't do this. She's a vindictive woman. Just ask poor Phil."

Jared made it a point not to take sides between Harper's warring parents, but when it came down to it, if he had to choose a favorite, Phil was going to win every day of the week. While the tempestuous man wasn't always thrilled with Jared's romantic overtures toward his daughter, he was still easier to get along with than Gloria, who seemed to be the lead conductor on the judgmental train.

"I can't see her doing this." Jared was firm. "I mean ... what's the point? She switches boyfriends like she does purses. She never keeps one for more than a few weeks. I couldn't even remember if I'd met this guy until Harper reminded me."

"She's still a suspect." Mel refused to back down. "I mean ... think about it. The fact that she was the one who discovered the body is enough to haul her in for questioning ... which is definitely something we're going to have to do."

Jared was uncomfortable with the sentiment. "What we need to do is go through his files," he corrected. "He's a divorce attorney. I'm betting he's alienated half the people in town just because of what he does for a living. It's far more likely the husband — or wife, for that matter — of a recent client did him in because he or she was upset regarding a financial settlement after a divorce."

"I guess that's possible." Mel didn't look convinced. "We'll have to get a warrant to go through the files. I doubt we're going to get that today. Until then, we can search the house for clues and let the medical examiner handle the body. After that, though ... ." He didn't finish the sentence. He didn't have to. Jared knew exactly what he wasn't saying, and it was a heckuva lot.

"I'm sure the suspect we're looking for is in the files." Jared hoped he sounded more certain than he felt. The more Mel talked, the more he wondered if Gloria would legitimately be considered a suspect. The idea terrified him for more than one reason. "Let's not jump to conclusions before it's necessary."

"Okay." Mel held up his hands in capitulation. "For now, we'll do things your way. We're still going to have to question Gloria because she found the body ... and I'm the one who needs to do it because you're engaged to her daughter. That makes you tainted goods as far as she's concerned in this investigation."

That was a position Jared was happy to take. "You can question her. Try not to be too aggressive until we know more. Harper will blow up if she thinks that you believe her mother is a murder suspect."

"I've got everything under control. This isn't my first time interviewing the relative of a friend. You have absolutely nothing to worry about."

Jared hoped that was true, but he couldn't make himself believe it.

Three

J ared and Mel focused on their work, taking a step back when the medical examiner's team entered and took over the scene. The man on duty was one they'd dealt with before. John Farber was the chief medical examiner and it was unusual for him to head out to a case ... especially in inclement weather.

"I'm surprised to see you," Mel noted as he watched the action from behind the couch. "How did you end up with this duty?"

"Half the staff called in because of the weather," Farber replied, his gaze grim as he studied Gibbons. "I don't think it's going to be hard to ascertain how he died. See this wound here." He indicated a messy spot to the upper left of the man's chest quadrant. "That's likely a direct blow to the heart. I'll have to make sure when I cut him open but that's my initial assumption."

Jared pursed his lips as he watched Farber's aides work. "Can you tell us anything else?"

Farber hiked an eyebrow. "Snow makes people crazy."

"Not *that*. I'm talking about the angle of the wounds. Do you think he was sitting down when he was attacked? Was he standing? Did the blows come from below?"

Mel cast his partner a sidelong look. "Those are all good questions. They can't be answered until he gets the body into the lab, though."

"That's very true," Farber agreed. "I don't know if he was attacked on the ground or not." He moved closer to the couch. "I don't see any blood spatter here, but that doesn't necessarily mean anything. It's a patterned couch and the pattern has some red in it."

Jared thought of the plaid couch he had at home and immediately started hating the fabric as much as Harper. "Well ... just keep us informed."

"That's the plan."

Jared and Mel moved toward the door in unison. Even though he wasn't looking forward to it, Jared knew what would come next. It was time to question Gloria ... and the conversation wouldn't be pleasant.

"Do you know anything?" Harper asked. She was hovering in the doorway and she almost pounced on Jared when he stepped through the opening.

"We know he's dead," Mel replied, earning a harsh look from the blonde. "We know he was stabbed multiple times. We need to get a warrant to go through his files, though, so that won't come through until tomorrow at the earliest."

"Oh." Harper moved closer to Jared. "What do you think?"

She was anxious, Jared realized. She wanted him to reassure her that Gloria wasn't a suspect. He wanted nothing more than to do that, but he'd promised never to lie to her ... and he wasn't about to start now.

"I don't know, Heart." His fingers were gentle when they brushed her flaxen hair away from her face. Between the dry air, their afternoon romp, and the snow that dampened her hair before entering the house, she looked as if she was boasting an extreme case of bedhead. Under different circumstances, it would've made him smile. Now, all he could do was avoid the question. "It's really too soon to say."

"My mother isn't a suspect, though, right?"

Jared involuntarily cringed. "We don't have suspects yet. You know how this works. We need more information. Heck, we need those files."

Harper wasn't placated, but she couldn't push him further. "Yeah, well, what comes next?"

"Mel has to ask your mother some questions."

"Mel?" She was instantly suspicious. "Why is Mel asking the questions?"

"Because it's inappropriate for me to do it given my relationship with you."

"But ... Mel has known my mother longer than you have," Harper argued. "Our families have been tight for a really long time."

"I understand that. I'm still engaged to you, which creates an issue. I can't be the one to interview her. I'm sorry. That's a strict rule. I couldn't interview you either."

"You did before."

"Before we were involved."

"But ... ." Harper made a frustrated sound deep in her throat. "I guess I understand it," she said after a beat. "I don't like it, but I understand it."

"Thank you." He brushed a kiss against her temple and then moved to the foyer so he could listen as Mel asked Gloria some very tough questions. For her part, Gloria seemed more together than before.

"How long have you been dating him, Gloria?" Mel asked, a notebook out as he jotted down her answers.

"Oh, I ... can't really remember."

"You *have* to remember." Mel was firm. "I doubt it's been long enough to explain forgetting."

"About a month," Harper automatically answered. "I think it was about five weeks ago when she told me she was done dating Anton – I never got to meet him and I'm sad because I liked his name – and she was dating Carl within a week or so. We all had dinner about three weeks ago. Maybe it was even a month ago now that I'm thinking about it."

"Okay." Mel's smile was benign. "That's very good. How would you say things have been going between you?"

"Obviously they were going well." Gloria's tone was snippy. "Why else would I be here if they weren't going well?"

"Gloria, you know we have to ask these questions. There's nothing personal about it. We have no choice."

"It feels as if you should have a choice," Gloria countered. "I mean ... you've known me for a very long time. I'm good friends with your sister. I practically raised Zander."

Harper snorted ... and then realized what she'd done when she earned a sharp look from her mother. She tried to cover it up with a cough, but it wasn't a masterful effort.

"I believe my sister raised Zander, although I'm not sure why anyone would want to take credit for him," Mel said dryly. "I still have to ask these questions, Gloria. If you're uncomfortable, you can call an attorney and meet us at the police station."

Gloria looked intrigued by the option, but Harper swooped in before she could answer either way.

"Oh, she doesn't need an attorney." Harper made a dismissive hand gesture. "It's not as if she's guilty. Just tell them what they want to hear, Mom. We'll make sure you get something to eat afterwards. You probably haven't eaten all day."

"Yes, well ... ." It was obvious Gloria wasn't happy with her daughter's insistence on answering the questions without legal representation. Gloria was a woman who liked to keep up appearances, though, and that's exactly what she did now. "What do you need to know?"

"I need to know the basics of your relationship," Mel replied without hesitation. "How close were you?"

"We'd only been dating a month like Harper told you," she replied. "I mean ... we were getting to know one another. I'm not sure how well it was going yet."

"So ... you weren't intimate, right?" Mel's cheeks burned, but he managed to maintain eye contact.

For her part, Gloria didn't even bother feigning embarrassment. "Oh, we were intimate. I don't believe in prolonging the inevitable if my partner is bad in bed. I mean ... if he has shortcomings, you know what I mean, I need to know that right away. I'm not the sort of woman who wants to waste her time."

Harper lowered her eyes and shook her head as Jared automatically moved his hand to her back. He'd known Gloria long enough to understand that she held nothing back when it came to talking about sex. She was open and free with the stories, which put Harper under a great deal of pressure and made Jared want to hide in a closet during her visits.

"Okay, so ... you were intimate." Mel flicked his eyes to Jared but found no help there. "How often were you spending the night together?"

"Oh, well ... he was in his fifties, which meant he couldn't go more than three times a week," Gloria explained. "I guess we basically saw each other on the odd days of the week."

"Meaning?"

"Tuesdays, Thursdays and Saturdays."

"What about Sundays?"

"Even the Lord rests on Sundays," Gloria replied, not missing a beat.

"Okay. Well ... that's lovely." Mel scratched the side of his nose and tried to regroup. "Tell me about Carl. What do you know about him?"

"He's a divorce lawyer."

"And?"

"And what? He's got all his own hair and only combs it over bald spots. As far as I can tell, he has all his own teeth. If he's got fakes in there, they're good, so I'm fine with that. He doesn't wear polyester suits. Only leather shoes will do. He's not married ... at least any longer. That's basically all I know about him. Oh, well, and he loves Italian food. I had to break him of eating that four times a week, though, because the garlic breath was outrageous."

Harper wanted to crawl into a hole and die, but she remained standing as Jared lent her a little bit of his strength.

"What do you know about his family? Did he have children?"

"He had at least one son. I didn't ask him about his family."

"You didn't ask him about his family?" Harper was mortified. "Mother, why would you date someone and not take the time to get to know him? I mean ... that's so rude. I'm sure you told him about me. Why wouldn't you sit and listen to him talk about his children?"

"I didn't tell him about you."

"You didn't?" Harper didn't know if she should be relieved or hurt. "Why?"

"Because you're almost thirty and I don't want to be the mother of a thirty-year-old single woman. It looks bad."

Jared shifted from one foot to the other, uncomfortable with the turn the conversation was taking. "We're getting married," he pointed out.

"That doesn't matter." Harper's frustration was obvious. "I don't see the problem with acting your own age. You're in your fifties, Mother. Why is that such a bad thing?"

"Carl thought I was forty-four."

Jared choked out a laugh before he realized that Gloria was glaring at him. "Oh, um ... ."

"There's no way he believed you were forty-four," Harper argued. "Come on. You look good, but you don't look that good."

"I moisturize," Gloria shot back. "I look amazing for my age. You should take a page out of my book before it's too late."

"I'll get right on that," Harper grumbled, shaking her head.

"You look fine," Jared reassured her. "Gloria, you need to focus on the questions Mel is asking. It's important."

"I'm answering them." Gloria's eyes fired with resentment. "I don't know what you want from me. We didn't know each other all that well. We spent a few nights a week together. I didn't hear from him yesterday, which was unusual, so I came over today to see what he was doing. The front door was unlocked so I let myself in ... and I found him in the living room."

"And that's it?" Mel queried.

"That's it."

"How long were you in the house before you found him?"

"Oh, not long." Gloria screwed up her face in concentration. "I'm guessing it was about three or four minutes. I checked the kitchen first because he's usually in there, but the living room was my second stop."

"And then what did you do?"

"I called Harper because I was freaked out. I knew she would be able to get Jared to come to the scene and my mind wasn't working very well on its own. I mean ... you saw it in there. It was horrible. I wasn't thinking clearly."

Jared thought about the snow he saw piled on Gloria's vehicle in the driveway. To him, that indicated she'd been in the house longer than she wanted to admit. The obvious question was on the tip of his tongue, but he couldn't make himself ask it.

"Okay, I guess that's all I need for now," Mel said. "I'm going to be in touch again, though. This isn't the end of it. There are other things we need to do before we question you again, though."

"Oh, well, I'm so looking forward to that." Disdain practically dripped from her tongue. "Come on, Harper. Let's get out of here. I believe you offered me dinner. I would like to make that happen."

"Oh, well, sure." Harper looked to Jared for help. "We can go to Zander's house. That's where we were going to eat tonight. He won't care if we add another hungry mouth."

"Whatever. I just want out of here. I'm utterly famished."

"You've had a rough day. I'm sure food will make you feel better."

JARED VOLUNTEERED TO RETURN to Carl's house once he dropped Harper off at Zander's place – he wasn't comfortable allowing her to ride with her mother, who insisted she was an expert at navigating the snow even though she had a small car and bad reflexes – but Mel told him it wasn't necessary. Until they got a warrant to go through Carl's files and had more information from the medical examiner to work with, there was absolutely no reason for Jared to stay. That was almost a disappointment for the small-town detective, especially since that meant he would have to sit through a meal with Gloria.

Zander and his boyfriend Shawn met the trio at the door and Zander was already pandering to Gloria when Jared slipped out of his coat and hung it on the over-the-top rack on the door.

"You poor thing," he cooed. "I can't believe you found a dead body today. That's horrible."

"I've found numerous dead bodies," Harper pointed out. "You never say it's bad when it happens to me."

"You're used to it," Zander shot back, causing Jared to smirk.

Ever helpful, Shawn helped Harper out of her coat as she looked around at the newly rearranged living room. "Your hands are cold. You should've remembered gloves when you were going out."

Harper ignored the admonishment. "What's going on here?" she asked, confused as she twirled. "Why does the living room look completely different from how it used to look?"

"Because we changed things," Zander replied without hesitation. "Shawn pointed out – and I agree – that the Feng Shui of the room was off. We decided to fix that."

"The Feng Shui?" Harper made a face. "I was the one who picked out how the room was laid out before."

"And now you don't live here," Zander reminded her. "You live across the street and have your own furniture to arrange. Although ... have you bought new furniture yet?" He directed the question to Jared, as if he was the one holding Harper back from having new things.

"We're working on it," Jared replied. "We were looking through catalogs when we got the call from Gloria."

"Oh, yes, it's my fault," Gloria drawled. "It's not as if you guys haven't had months to pick out furniture. Me discovering a body is obviously the worst thing that happened to *you* today."

Jared glared at her. "Listen here ... ."

Harper put a hand on his arm to still him. "Please don't make things worse," she whispered, her eyes open and pleading. "I can't take it if you do that. I'm serious."

He growled out a noise but maintained control. "We're getting furniture. In fact, we'll have it before you know it."

"I think you should let me loose to pick out the furniture," Gloria argued. "I'll have that place decked out in two weeks flat if you let me have control."

"I think Jared and I would prefer maintaining control of our own home," Harper argued. "Besides, you have other things to worry about ... like your dead boyfriend. I still can't believe you discovered him like that."

"I can't either." Gloria made a clucking sound with her tongue. "I mean ... it's the absolute worst. I'll have nightmares because of it. I won't be able to sleep in my own home because of the fear."

"Was it bad?" Shawn asked, directing the question to Jared.

"It was bad," he confirmed. "It was ... an unfortunate scene."

"Word on the street is that he was stabbed so many times Norman Bates is jealous," Zander supplied.

Jared frowned. "Um ... how can you possibly know that?"

"Because Mel was supposed to have dinner with my mother and canceled and that's what he told her."

"Oh, well ... ."

Zander didn't want for Jared to respond. "Do you know what you should do, Gloria? You should move in with Jared and Harper for a bit. They've got a guest room and need help decorating and you're afraid to stay by yourself. It's best for all of you."

If looks could kill, Zander would be dead.

Jared uncomfortably cleared his throat. "Um ... I don't think that's a good idea," he hedged. "I mean, we barely have a bed in the spare room. It doesn't even have bedding on it. Like ... there are no sheets or pillows."

"Oh, I can handle that." Gloria appeared thrilled with the suggestion. "I think it's a fine idea. It will give me something to focus on besides the horror that my life has become."

Harper felt put upon, but she didn't see where she had much of a choice. "We would love for you to stay with us tonight."

"Great."

"Just one night," Harper stressed. "I'm sure you'll be feeling better tomorrow."

"We'll play it by ear."

Four

J ared was up a full hour before Harper woke, but he remained still so she could sleep. His mind was busy with possibilities ... and none of them were good.

The more he thought about it, the more he wondered if Gloria was capable of murder. He tried to line up what he knew about the woman and realized it was precious little.

She was in the middle of a contentious divorce that seemed to be going nowhere. In fact, since he'd met Harper — and that was almost ten months ago — he'd seen no movement on the divorce. As far as he could tell, Phil and Gloria Harlow enjoyed making each other miserable so there was no reason to divorce. They were getting exactly what they wanted out of the current predicament.

She was a passive-aggressive nightmare, meaning she enjoyed messing with Harper's mind whenever she stopped by. She was the sort of woman who thought other women got their self-worth from the men they were dating. Harper didn't believe that and held firm when Gloria started bandying about relief regarding the fact that her daughter was finally dating someone and not going to be alone for the rest of her life.

Gloria was a woman who liked fine clothing, shoes, dishes, and furniture. She was willing to pay more for name brand items. She liked expensive purses — Jared was pretty sure Harper only had one purse and rarely carried it — and she even wore a fur stole in the winter months, which Harper found abhorrent.

She liked to argue with Harper, wear her down at times. So far, Jared hadn't voiced his concern about this tendency, but he was gearing up for it now that he and Harper were planning their wedding. There was no way he would allow Gloria to steamroll Harper when it came to picking the venue and dress.

Other than that, Jared realized he knew very little about the woman, and he found it troubling.

"Are you up?" Harper's voice was sleepy as she stretched.

"I am." He pressed a kiss to her forehead as she snuggled closer. He relished this time with her. Quiet mornings were a favorite part of his day. The fact that he was worried he would soon be arresting her mother only made him more desperate to embrace this morning, when time felt somehow precious.

"How did you sleep?"

That was a loaded question, Jared mused. "I slept okay." He shifted his eyes to the window. "It's stopped snowing."

"That's good." She kissed his strong jaw. "I can hear your busy brain from here. Do you want to tell me what you're thinking?"

"I'm thinking that I love you." The response was easy ... and true. "What are you thinking?"

"That you're mad because my mother spent the night."

He stilled, surprised. "I don't care about that," he said finally. "Er, well, I'm not happy about it exactly. I'm not mad about it either. I understand why you wanted her here."

"Oh, I didn't want her here." Harper made a hysterical face that caused Jared's lips to quirk. "This place is a mess. It's basically a nonstop way for her to criticize me. I was hoping she wouldn't visit until spring. She's like a bear in some ways. She likes to hunker down and hibernate for the winter."

"That explains the fur coat."

She laughed, the sound warming Jared to his toes. "I hate that coat."

"I know you do." He ran his hand over her hair to smooth it. "We should probably get up. For all we know, she's out there rearranging our kitchen."

"We only have four glasses, five plates, and plastic forks. She's not going to take that well."

"I don't care." He tipped up her chin so he could stare into her eyes. "I only care what we like ... and I happen to like you best."

Her eyes sparkled. "I like you best, too. Although ... don't tell Zander."

"Your secret is safe with me."

GLORIA INDEED WAS KNEE-DEEP IN the cupboards when Jared and Harper finished showering and dressing in their master suite.

"Where is your good china?" she asked by way of greeting when she stood and fixed them with expectant looks.

Harper merely shrugged. "At your house until you die."

Jared choked on the coffee he'd just poured, his cheeks turning a bright shade of red.

"Very funny, dear." Gloria was blasé as she glanced around the room. "Why don't you have real dishes?"

"Because we haven't picked any out yet." Harper accepted the mug of coffee Jared slid in her direction. "It's not a big deal. That's actually low on our list of things we're worried about right now. Furniture is first."

"Furniture is definitely a thing," Gloria agreed, wiping off her hands on the apron she'd tied around her waist.

"Where did you get that?" Harper was focused on the apron, confused. "I didn't have that."

"I borrowed it from Zander this morning. By the way, he's already up and working. He says he's going into the office later if you need to get in touch with him. Apparently you guys don't have clients right now. He didn't say as much, but I know how to read him. Do you think it's wise for you to go so long between clients?"

Harper pursed her lips. "Well ... I can't exactly force ghosts to show up, can I? I'm not magical. They make themselves known when they feel like it."

"I think you're magical," Jared whispered as he brushed his lips against the ridge of her ear.

Gloria ignored the display of unabashed affection. "I think we should spend the day shopping."

The announcement was enough to cause Harper's blood to chill. "Oh, well ... ."

"Harper and I want to shop together," Jared supplied. He wasn't afraid of butting heads with Gloria. He would take the brunt of her unhappiness if it became necessary because he wanted to shield Harper from her mother's attitude. "She can't buy things unless we both agree on them."

Harper shot him a grateful look. "The shopping has to wait until Jared and I can do it together."

"Fine." Gloria's glare was pronounced when it landed on Jared. "I guess we'll just do what Jared wants."

"Oh, if only we lived in that sort of world," he drawled, grinning when Harper's eyes went wide. "I should probably get going, Heart. I need to start my day. I'm betting it's going to be a long one thanks to that storm."

"Okay." She briefly rested her hand on his chest, causing him to place his hand over it and meet her gaze. "Will you call me if you learn anything important?"

He nodded. "Yeah. I don't want you sitting around worrying." He finished his coffee and stepped forward so he could hug her. "Hopefully we'll be able to get into Gibbons's files before the end of the day. That will be a great help."

"I'm sure one of those degenerates is the guilty party," Gloria said.

"That would be nice," Jared agreed. "I ... ." He didn't get a chance to finish what he was going to say because the front door flew open to allow Phil entrance. He barreled through the house without calling out a greeting and pointed himself directly toward the kitchen.

"What is this I hear about you being a murderer, Gloria?" His expression was hard to read, but Jared sensed things were about to turn ugly.

"And I think that's my cue to flee." Jared gave Harper another quick kiss. "Hide in the bedroom if things get too rough."

Harper grabbed the front of his shirt to stop him from running. "You cannot leave me to deal with this on my own," she hissed. "I'm not equipped to handle a situation of this magnitude."

"They're your parents."

"That's why I know I'm out of my depth."

"Well ... I can't help you." Jared ran his hands up and down her arms to soothe her. "This one is all on you. I have to get to the office."

"But ... what about breakfast?" Harper was grasping at straws now. "Don't you want me to cook you breakfast?"

"It is the most important meal of the day," Gloria agreed pointedly.

"I'll pick up something on the way. I need to get moving." Jared was firm as he moved his coffee cup to the dishwasher before giving the three people in the kitchen a serious look. "Try not to kill each other. Oh, and if you do decide death is warranted, stay away from Harper. You guys can kill each other all you want. She's not to be touched."

Gloria's gaze was withering. "Oh, well, you're just a laugh a minute, aren't you?"

"I moonlight as a comedian in my spare time."

Gloria flicked her eyes to Harper. "I'm not sure what you see in him. Is it his looks? If so, we can probably find you someone else who looks almost as good as him. Although ... have you ever considered dating a short man? They're usually so grateful just to be allowed in the game they'll do whatever you want."

Harper bit back a sigh. "Let's cook breakfast, Mom. After that we'll ... do something."

"I DON'T UNDERSTAND HOW THIS happened," Phil lamented as he sat at the dining room table and watched his daughter and estranged wife buzz around the kitchen. "How did you get yourself in the middle of such a mess, Gloria?"

For her part, Gloria was busy pretending she wasn't bothered by the previous day's events. She was a fine actress, but even she was having trouble with this performance. "It's not my fault," she complained as she watched Harper flip hash browns in a skillet. "Do you really buy potatoes in a bag like that? I don't understand why you can't just make them from scratch like you're supposed to. That's what a real cook does."

"I'm a ghost hunter, not a cook," Harper reminded her. "I happen to like hash browns in a bag. They make things so much easier."

"If you say so." Gloria was obviously dubious. "As for what happened with Carl, it's honestly not my fault. I thought he was a catch. Apparently I was wrong."

"Apparently?" Phil arched an eyebrow. "I would think that you were definitely wrong."

"Don't fight," Harper warned, waving the spatula. "I can't deal with you guys fighting right now. I mean it."

"We're not going to fight," Phil reassured her.

"We're not?" Gloria didn't look so sure. "If we don't fight, we have absolutely nothing to talk about."

"We need to talk about your defense plan," Phil stressed. "I mean ... who is your attorney?"

Gloria knit her eyebrows together. "I don't believe I need an attorney."

"Oh, you need an attorney." Phil was having none of it. "If you don't have an attorney, you're going to prison for the rest of your life. I mean ... you killed a man. You can't just get away with that."

"Dad, she didn't kill anyone," Harper argued. "She just found the body."

Phil looked to Gloria for confirmation. "Is that true or is Harper just being Harper?"

"What is that supposed to mean?" Harper made a protesting sound as she swiveled. "I happen to think that it's good to be like me."

"Of course it is." Phil graced his only child with a patient look. It was something from his repertoire that he couldn't generate for anyone else, especially his estranged wife. "You're the sunshine of my life, kid."

Harper beamed at him.

"You're also naive." He was firm when her mouth dropped open.

"You don't like to see the bad about your mother. She's very likely the prime suspect in this murder."

"That's not true," Gloria sputtered, her fury on full display. "I am not a suspect. If I was a suspect, I would be in jail."

"Not if they're still collecting evidence." Phil was matter-of-fact. "I'm being serious, Gloria. You're the one who found the body. That means you're the prime suspect."

"Says who?"

"Says anyone who has ever paid attention to an investigation. I mean ... don't you watch *Dateline*? For crying out loud. The person who discovers the body is always the prime suspect."

Gloria's eyes were wide and full of fright when she turned them to Harper. "Is that true?"

Harper didn't know how to answer. "I don't know." She swallowed hard as she ran the possibility through her head. Jared had once mentioned something very similar to her. She hadn't remembered it until her father brought it up ... and now she was terrified. "I think Jared would've told me if Mom was a suspect."

"Oh, you poor thing." Phil patted her shoulder and made a clucking sound with his tongue. "You haven't put this together yet. I'm not surprised."

"It's not that." Harper's temper fired on all cylinders. "I'm not an idiot. You're talking about me like I'm an idiot."

"Of course you're not an idiot. You're a gifted girl. You don't see the evil in others ... like your mother."

"I'm not evil!" Gloria snapped. "I didn't kill Carl. I mean ... why would I? That's the stupidest thing I've ever heard."

"And yet the news spreading about town is that you caught him cheating on you and cut off his junk," Phil argued.

"Cut off his ... ." Gloria's face drained of color. "Who would dare share that lie?"

Phil averted his gaze. "I forget who I heard it from."

"Oh, you didn't forget." Gloria was beside herself. "How can you possibly believe I would kill someone? That is just ridiculous."

"I've met you." Phil adopted a pragmatic tone. "I know what you're capable of."

"Exactly."

"You're definitely capable of murder." He refused to back down as Gloria made a series of wounded animal noises deep in her throat. "We need to get ahead of this. That means you need a lawyer ... and I'm not sure who will take you on given the fact that you've dated every lawyer in the area. You might have to tap someone from out of state."

Harper was flummoxed as she moved the skillet from the heat and tried to wrap her head around what her father was saying. "You don't really think she's going to be arrested, do you?"

"Harper, your mother was dating the man in question and she found the body. Who else are they going to arrest?"

"The guilty party."

"We both know your mother is very likely the guilty party."

"You take that back!" Gloria jabbed a finger into Phil's chest and glared at him. "I'm not a murderer. The fact that you can say something like that just proves how terrible a fit we really were."

"I couldn't agree more." Phil was solemn. "That's neither here nor there, though. You need an attorney and it's going to be difficult to find you one because you refuse to stop sleeping with every entry on the Michigan Bar Association's website."

"Oh, stuff it!" Gloria graced him with the darkest glare in her repertoire. "If you're not careful, I'll take you out and we'll see if you're so full of yourself then, won't we?"

Harper stirred. "That's a point right there," she said. "If Mom was a killer, why wouldn't she just take you out? She hates you."

"We share a child," Phil replied simply. "Women don't kill the men who fathered their children unless the children are at risk. I saw it on *Oprah* once. It's a real thing. Your mother took all the rage she was feeling for me and pointed it at Carl because she couldn't kill me. This is standard psychiatry."

Harper pressed the heel of her hand to her forehead as she struggled to maintain her cool. "Well, that is ... something to think about."

"It's going to be brought up at trial, so we definitely need to think about it," Phil agreed. "I suggest we call Donnie Lakeland out of Sterling Heights. He used to be an Oakland County attorney and I'm pretty sure that your mother hasn't worked her way up to him yet."

"I definitely haven't slept with him," Gloria agreed. "He was out of the office when I stopped by."

"See." Phil was awfully blasé for a guy who was trying to help the woman he hated most avoid a murder conviction. "We should call him."

"We're not going to call him," Harper snapped, her eyes busy as she considered a bevy of possibilities. "In fact ... yeah, I've got a better idea."

"You do?" Phil fixed his daughter with a dubious look. "I thought you didn't believe she was going to be arrested."

"I don't. Jared would've told me if she was a suspect."

"Not unless he wanted to break your heart and that's the last thing he wants to do. He's good that way."

"I was just thinking this morning that she could do better," Gloria countered. "I think she should move back in with Zander and put Jared behind her."

"And I think you're dreaming if you believe she's going to do that," Phil said. "Good grief. Stop focusing on what you want and start considering what's best for your daughter. In this particular instance, that's Jared."

"I don't happen to believe that."

"And I don't care what either of you believes," Harper exploded, her temper finally making an appearance. "Talk about Jared is off the table. He's part of my life and that's never going to change." For emphasis, she wagged the fingers on her left hand to show off the engagement ring.

"Now, I still think the best thing to do is solve the crime," she continued. "That will prove Mom isn't guilty."

"And how do you suggest we do that?" Gloria queried, legitimately curious.

"We find Carl's ghost."

"Can you do that?"

"That's what I do for a living."

"I know but ... I've never seen you in action."

"Then you're in for a treat." Harper was determined as she started doling out hash browns on plates. "We'll have breakfast and then find

Carl's ghost. That's definitely the plan for today."

"And when that fails we'll call Donnie Lakeland," Phil said. "He'll help us get out of this mess."

Harper could do nothing but growl in the face of endless hours with her parents. This was so not how she planned to spend her day.

Five

M el was in the interrogation room with a woman when Jared arrived at the station. Since he wasn't sure what to do, Jared ate his McDonald's breakfast at his desk and waited until Mel motioned for him to join the party.

"This is Cheryl Wagner," he said by way of introduction.

Jared shook the woman's hand and took the open seat next to his partner. "Hello."

"She's one of Carl Gibbons's former clients," Mel explained. "She heard about his death on the news and has some information for us."

Jared brightened considerably. Any suspect that wasn't Gloria was cause for celebration. "Really?"

The woman, a pretty blonde in her forties, bobbed her head. "Yes. Carl was my attorney when I divorced my ex-husband. He was a shark, which David didn't like. That's my ex, by the way. David Wagner. He's the scum of the earth."

Jared kept his expression neutral. "Are you saying you believe your ex-husband killed Carl?"

"Most definitely. He threatened Carl with castration when the mediator came back with the settlement numbers."

Jared exchanged a quick look with Mel. Gibbons was stabbed, not castrated. Still, it was a solid lead. "You're probably going to have to start from the beginning."

"There's not much to tell," Cherry replied on a shrug. "I found out that David was cheating on me with his secretary. I knew something was going on with them for months before I finally confronted him. He didn't even bother denying it. He said that it was a side thing and I shouldn't worry about it."

"How did you react to that?"

"How do you think? I told him I was going to take every dime he ever made. That's why I got Carl as my attorney. I put a retainer down before I even confronted David because I wanted to make sure that I had the best attorney in the area already locked down before he could try to get Carl on his side."

"Was Gibbons considered the best divorce attorney in the area?" Jared queried.

"Oh, most definitely." Cheryl's smile was smug. "He always wins. I still remember the look on David's face when I told him I'd already retained Carl as my attorney. He was furious, said he would end the affair and we could go back to the way things were. It was far too late for that."

Jared was officially intrigued. "And how much money did you get out of your ex-husband in the divorce?"

"I got half of everything even though he tried to hide assets. I got the house ... and his BMW ... and I got the kids. He has to pay two grand a month in child support, which he freaked out about because the kids are both teenagers now. It was really funny."

Cheryl seemed to be reveling in her storytelling, which Jared found uncomfortable. He couldn't imagine loving someone enough to marry him or her and then essentially throwing a party when that relationship fell apart. He had no intention of ever letting anything like that happen with Harper. As far as he was concerned, he was marrying for life. He knew she felt the same way.

"And what makes you think David would actually follow through on his threat?" Mel pressed. "I would guess that people say a lot of things they don't really mean in the heat of a divorce. I've never personally been through the process, but I've heard horror stories through the years. Most of the time, if violence is to occur, it happens right away. Your divorce has been finalized for months."

"David is smart," Cheryl replied without hesitation. "He knows all too well that he would be the prime suspect if he didn't wait. He was still grumbling about what Carl managed to pull off last time I saw him."

"And when was that?"

"About two weeks ago, he was dropping off my daughter's backpack because she forgot it at his apartment. Oh, he has to live in an apartment now because he can't afford a house. His young secretary girlfriend dumped him because he can't shower her with gifts, too. I know about that because my son told me. I guess David was ranting and raving."

"Well, that sounds ... terrible." Jared rubbed his chin, considering. "What precise threats did your ex-husband make?"

"He said he was going to cut off Carl's testicles and feed them to him," Cheryl replied. "He was convinced Carl and I had something going on, which was ridiculous because ... have you seen his hair? You can see his scalp through it and he used a pen to darken some areas to hide it. I would never date a guy who did that."

"Were you having an affair?" Mel asked the woman pointedly. "It's important that you tell the truth."

"I had no interest in having an affair." Cheryl appeared earnest. "I wanted the money. I don't care if I ever have another relationship. David broke my heart ... and I paid him back. Those were the things I cared about.

"As far as I'm concerned, everything turned out exactly how I wanted it to turn out," she continued. "Carl had a reputation for sleeping with clients, but I told him that was off the table from the start. He was fine with that as long as he got his payment. That's all there was to it."

"Okay, well ... we might have more questions at a later time." Mel's gaze was heavy when it locked with his partner's conflicted orbs. "For now, we're going to question David and see what he has to say."

"Oh, I would love to be a fly on the wall for that conversation."

. . .

DAVID WAGNER WAS A CPA AT an accounting firm in New Baltimore. Jared and Mel headed to his office right after wrapping up their interview with Cheryl. Both of them were flummoxed by the turn of events.

"How was Harper last night?" Mel asked as they exited the cruiser in the parking lot. "Did she ask questions about her mother?"

"Yeah, but I deflected them as much as possible."

"You don't want to tell her the truth?"

"That her mother is a murder suspect? No, I don't want to tell her that."

"I think you should."

"And I think you should mind your own business." Jared fought hard to tamp down his anger. "It will upset her."

"Harper is a big girl." Mel wasn't the sort to back down under normal circumstances and he certainly wasn't going to start now. "It will be better for her over the long haul if you tell her the truth now."

"There is no truth to tell. Her mother isn't our prime suspect right now."

"She's not," Mel agreed. "I don't want you focusing on David Wagner to the detriment of common sense to make sure that stays true, though. Can you promise me that?"

Jared was offended. "Do you really think I would frame a guy to keep Harper happy?"

"I think there's very little you wouldn't do to protect Harper. You can't save her from this if Gloria is a murderer, though. You have to realize that."

The problem was, Jared realized exactly that. The realization was eating at him. "We don't know anything yet," he pointed out. "There's no sense getting her worked up until we have an actual direction to look."

"If you say so."

"Well ... I say so."

Jared was morose as he followed his partner into the building. It was a three-story brick facade with multiple windows and zero personality. The detectives stopped at the front desk to talk to the secretary, who was young and blonde. She batted her eyelashes at Jared as they waited for David to come to the lobby to collect them.

"You live in Whisper Cove?" she asked.

Mel knew she wasn't talking to him, but he answered anyway. "We do."

"I've always liked Whisper Cove. It's ... cool." She twirled a strand of hair around her finger as she regarded Jared with flirty eyes. "What do you do in Whisper Cove for fun?"

Jared was in no mood for games. "Spend time with my fiancée."

"Oh." Disappointment practically flowed off the young woman in waves. "That's a bummer."

"Not from my perspective."

Thankfully for both men, David picked that moment to save them from an unfortunate conversation. He looked tired, dark circles under his eyes, and he seemed confused why the police would want to see him.

"Can I help you?"

"David Wagner?" Mel asked, flashing his badge.

"Yes."

"We're with the Whisper Cove Police Department. We have a few questions to ask you regarding your relationship with Carl Gibbons."

Surprise washed over David's features — and a momentary glint of hatred — but he recovered quickly. "I see. Um ... come into my office." He flicked his eyes to the blonde. "Sassy, hold my calls."

The girl shot him a withering look. "Whatever you say, *Mr. Wagner.*"

Jared had no doubt that Sassy — seriously, who named their kid that? — was the secretary Cheryl mentioned when talking about her husband's affair. They clearly had a history ... and it wasn't one that was full of roses and puppies.

David didn't speak again until Mel and Jared were seated in his office. He offered them refreshments, which they politely declined, and then turned to business. "If this is about something Cheryl said ... ."

"What makes you think she's the one who sent us here?" Mel queried.

"We have what you would call a tempestuous relationship."

Jared figured that was a mild word for what these former lovers felt for each other. "We're here to ask about your history with Carl Gibbons," he supplied. "It's our understanding that you didn't like him."

"Would you like the man who basically bankrupted you?" David challenged. "I hate that guy. I make no bones about it. If he filed a complaint about the letter I sent him ... well ... I'm still not sorry. I meant everything I said in that letter. He's a total bottom-feeder."

Jared exchanged a quick look with Mel and then adjusted his tack. "Sir, are you aware that Mr. Gibbons was murdered in his home yesterday?"

David's face went slack. "W-what?"

"He's dead," Jared repeated. "He was stabbed inside his home."

"Are you kidding?"

"We don't generally make jokes about murder," Mel replied dryly.

"I see." David steepled his fingers on his desk and then burst out laughing. It wasn't the reaction Jared was expecting. "Oh, this is the best thing that's happened in ... I don't know how long. Please tell me he didn't die right away. Did he linger? Did he suffer?"

Jared was caught off guard by the CPA's bloodthirsty reaction. "We don't have the full medical examiner's report yet. That seems unlikely, though."

"What a bummer."

Mel cleared his throat to get David's attention. "You realize you're a suspect in his murder because of your recent threats against him, right?"

The smile disappeared from David's face. "What threats? I didn't make any threats."

"So ... you didn't threaten to castrate the victim and feed his testicles to him?" Jared asked.

"Oh, *that*." David rolled his eyes, hard. "That was just normal venting. I didn't really mean it. Do you have any idea how much money that guy cost me? Of course I was going to threaten him. He had it coming. He didn't even seem bothered by it."

"I don't think threatening to castrate someone is normal," Mel countered.

"Then you obviously haven't been divorced." David was back to smiling. "There's nothing to get worked up about. I said that, but I didn't follow-through. I mean ... what would be the point? It's not as if killing him would get my money back. That's all I care about."

His words made sense, which caused the ball of despair taking up residence in the pit of Jared's stomach to return with a vengeance. "We're still going to need to know your whereabouts last night."

"What time?"

"Between ten and four."

"That's a big window."

"We'll be able to narrow it down later this afternoon. If you prefer waiting until then, that's your prerogative."

"It doesn't matter." David leaned back in his chair and smirked. "For the first time since getting divorced, I feel lucky. I'm covered for all that time last night because I was with a woman."

Jared pictured the secretary. "Sassy?"

"Oh, no. She dumped me when she realized Cheryl took all my money. It turns out she was only interested in me buying things for her. Go figure. I was with another woman."

"And who might that be?"

"Sally Beaufort. She's Sassy's mother. I don't think Sassy knows yet. I'm looking forward to her finding out, though."

Mel gulped down his disgust. "And you were with her all night?"

"I was." He bobbed his head. "It went well enough that I'm seeing her again tonight. Go ahead and give her a call. I have nothing to hide."

"We'll check out your alibi." Mel turned his rueful gaze to Jared, sympathy for his fellow detective's plight rushing through him. "I'm sure we'll be in touch."

"I'm looking forward to it."

HARPER WAS IN A PICKLE WHEN she landed on the street in front of Gibbons's house. Police tape covered the front door, a stark warning that she wasn't to enter the premises, but the ghost was most likely inside if he'd remained behind so she needed to cross the threshold if she expected to find him.

"Well, that sucks," she muttered as her mother and father joined her on the sidewalk.

"What's wrong?" Gloria readjusted her fur coat so the shoulders were square. "Do you see him already? If so, tell him I'm very mad at him."

"Oh, tell him I'm mad at him, too," Phil intoned. "He should've watched himself better so we wouldn't have to deal with this crap."

Harper rolled her eyes and pinched the bridge of her nose to ward off an oncoming headache. "Why did you insist on coming with us again, Dad? It's not that I'm not thrilled to be spending time with you or anything, but I am curious why you're here. It doesn't make a lot of sense to me."

Phil shot her a look. "If I'm not here, who is going to babysit the two of you? I don't really care if your mother gets in over her head. You're my daughter, though. It's my job to take care of you."

"Since when?" Harper muttered under her breath.

"I heard that." Phil extended a warning finger. "I don't need your lip, young lady. I was a good father to you. I went to all your school events ... and helped you with homework ... and took you fishing after your grandfather passed because you insisted it was necessary."

That was true, Harper realized. He did all those things. He also grilled any boy who had the guts to date her in high school, insisted she hide what she could do in case people laughed and pointed, and once threatened her with an asylum when she insisted they had a ghost living in their basement. That was true, although thankfully the ghost grew tired of listening to the elder Harlows fight and moved to a different house for some peace and quiet.

"I'm sorry." She held up her hands in mock capitulation as her father glared at her. "I wasn't trying to be difficult. It's just ... we're making a spectacle of ourselves." She pointed toward a set of moving curtains across the road. "I'm pretty sure we have an audience."

Gloria's forehead wrinkled as she stared at the lacy curtains. "That's Annette Foster's house. She's a busybody. Who cares what she thinks?"

Harper found the question hilarious because her mother was the queen of caring what other people thought. "I think we should adjust our tones." Harper was firm. "We don't want to draw unnecessary attention to ourselves."

"The solution to that is going inside," Phil suggested. "If we're off the street, nobody will be looking at us."

"I'm with you on that," Gloria said. "Let's get out of this cold."

Harper snagged her mother's arm before the woman could break any additional laws. "You can't cross the police tape. We can be arrested if you try."

"Oh, that's preposterous. I have a key."

"It's still a crime scene."

"I don't understand," Phil said, his hands landing on his hips. "Why did we come out here if it's not to head inside and talk to a ghost?"

"We need to lure the ghost outside," Harper replied. "We can't go inside. Annette will call the cops if she sees us crossing that tape and Jared won't be happy if he has to arrest me. That hasn't happened since that first time and he still gets irritated when I bring it up."

"That's because he's a whiner," Gloria supplied. "You shouldn't hitch yourself to a whiner forever, Harper. That never ends well. I should know." She cast a pointed look in Phil's direction.

"At least I'm not a murderer," Phil shot back. "This whiner will be here in a few years when our first grandchild is born. I'll be the one spending time with him or her — or them, most likely, since I think Harper and Jared are the types to have more than one child — and they won't know who you are. You'll just be that woman who is in prison for killing a divorce attorney."

"Stop saying that!" Gloria's eyes filled with fury. "I'm going to make you cry if you don't stop saying things like that."

"You've already made me cry quite enough for one lifetime."

Desperate to tune them out, Harper focused her attention on Gibbons's side yard. She was almost positive she saw a hint of movement behind a bush at one point and she decided to focus there ... because anything was better than listening to her parents carry on.

"I'm the one who did the crying, Phil," Gloria argued. "You were a horrible husband."

"I was a catch compared to you," Phil groused. "You were the devil in Prada heels. I mean … seriously. Why won't God just smite you and put you out of your misery?"

Harper ignored the sniping and moved toward the big bush that hid most of Gibbons's backyard. She was certain now that she'd seen movement and she was hopeful that movement belonged to a ghost. Otherwise, she was going to have to drink her lunch … and that wasn't a pretty picture.

"Where are you going?" Phil called out.

"I think he's over here. You guys keep arguing over there. I'll be back in a minute." And, with that, Harper disappeared into the backyard and came face to face with a dead man.

Six

Harper was so thankful for a few moments of silence she didn't bother looking over her shoulder to see if her parents were following. It seemed like too much effort.

She was barely around the bush when she practically tripped through Carl's ghost, who was watching her with eyes the size of saucers.

"*Oomph.*"

Harper slammed into a tree, although she was thankful for it because that meant she wouldn't hit the ground, which was cold and frozen thanks to the storm.

"Are you okay?" Carl reached out to help her and frowned when his hands passed through her body. "Oh, dear."

"That about sums it up," Harper grumbled as she rubbed her cheek. She could feel a sore spot and was worried it would develop into a bruise she would have trouble explaining to Jared.

"You're dead," Carl announced. He appeared relatively calm when delivering the words. "I'm sorry, my dear. You were so young." He pressed his hand to his heart and looked to the sky, as if praying.

"I'm not dead," Harper countered. "You're dead."

"No, you're definitely dead. My hands went right through you."

"They did, but it's because you're dead and can't touch the living. Wait ... that kind of sounds dirty when I think about it. Scratch that. Let's not talk about touching each other."

Carl ignored the outburst. He had other things on his mind. "I most certainly am not dead." He looked to a spot over Harper's shoulder and brightened considerably. "Here comes someone who will prove it to you. Oh, Gloria." He adopted a smarmy smile. "Will you please tell this adorable, and sadly dead, young lady that I'm alive?"

Gloria, of course, couldn't see him so she didn't respond. "Harper, you should announce when you're going to take a detour through the snow." She gestured toward her pants, which were covered with powdery white flakes. "My pants are now wet. You know how I feel about wet pants."

"Yes, the same way she feels about doing the dishes," Phil muttered.

"Gloria," Carl sang out. "I'm talking to you."

Harper almost felt sorry for him when her mother continued ranting at her rather than him.

"Why are we wading through the snow? I don't like it. I'm already cold ... and my coat is very unhappy."

Harper let loose a weary sigh. "I hate it when you pretend your coat has feelings, Mother."

"It does."

"Yes, but that just reminds me that it used to be made up of living animals."

"So did your suede boots."

Since she had a point, Harper decided to move on with the conversation. "Carl is here. I need you to shut up for a minute. We're having a conversation."

Gloria frowned. "He's here?" She glanced around, as if searching for proof. "Where?"

Harper pointed toward him. "He's upset. He thought I was dead and now he realizes it was him."

"Why would you be dead?"

"He was just confused."

"Well, frankly, that's rude." She adopted a stern expression as she stared at the empty spot. "You need to tell Harper who killed you, Carl. It's very important."

For his part, the already muddled ghost seemed more confused than ever. "I can't be dead," he complained, frustration positively wafting off him. "It's impossible. I have too much life left to live."

"I'm sorry." Harper tried to paste an earnest expression on her face, but it was so cold she had no doubt she woefully failed. "I do need you to try to think about your death, though. It's important. What's the last thing you remember?"

"Thinking you were a ghost," Carl snapped. "I was crushed by the thought, too. It's not often a hot chick sneaks into my backyard. I thought maybe we could do ghostly stuff together and Gloria would be none the wiser."

Harper made a face. "That is really gross."

"How is it gross? It's not really cheating if one of the people is dead. Speaking of that ... can I still do stuff?"

Harper's stomach turned. "Are you joking?"

"No. Why? Does it sound like I'm joking? I really want to know. Your answer could end up being extremely important to me."

Harper pursed her lips, disdain evident on her frigid features. "You realize that she's my mother, right?"

Carl was taken aback. "No. I ... no." He frowned. "Wait a second ... how could she be your mother? She's only forty-four. Are you the girl I met at dinner? I'm trying to remember. I don't think I paid much attention. She must've had you when she was in middle school."

Harper often wanted to throttle her mother. The inclination was doubly strong today. "She's not forty-four."

"Don't tell him that," Gloria barked. "My age is nobody's business."

"He's dead, Gloria," Phil pointed out. "Who is he going to tell?"

"Who knows? Maybe he'll tell the other ghosts and they'll write it in the fog on mirrors or something. I've seen that happen in ghost movies. I know because I watched a bunch of them when Harper's little ... gift ... first reared its ugly head."

Harper tried to pretend she couldn't hear her mother. "Let's talk about you, Carl," she prodded. "You're the most important person here this afternoon. We're all here for you."

"I don't really care about him," Phil argued. "I'm here because I didn't want to be left out ... and I was bored. It's winter. There's nothing to do in winter when it's too cold to go out on my boat."

"Who is that?" Carl asked, tilting his head.

"My father," Harper replied automatically.

Carl's mouth dropped open. "You charlatan!"

Harper glanced over her shoulder, confused. "Who are you talking to?"

"I knew you weren't completely over your ex," he seethed, glaring at Gloria. "I mean ... look at you. I'm barely cold in the ground and you're already running around with him."

"She's not running around with him," Harper argued. "I mean ... she is. It's not like that, though. Everyone was at my house and we decided to go on a ghost hunt together."

"Oh, likely story." Carl glared at his former girlfriend, who appeared more agitated about being out in the cold than she was about his death. "I knew getting involved with you was a mistake." He tried to wave his hand in her face, although Harper couldn't decide what he was trying to accomplish with the endeavor. "I hope you get crow's feet that can't be Botoxed away. Also, you don't look forty-four. I was lying when I told you that."

"What did he say?" Gloria asked.

Harper thought about telling her, but it would simply open another can of worms so she decided to sidestep the issue. "He seems upset. He might not be able to tell us who murdered him just yet. I think we're going to need to give him a minute."

"Oh, joy," Phil lamented. "There's nothing better than a ghost with memory issues."

THANKS TO THE STORY BREAKING BIG in the local news cycle, Jared and Mel returned to the office to find another walk-in.

This one's name was Morris Chesterfield, and he was a big ball of fury when the detectives got a chance to sit down with him.

"I want to know about the disposition of Carl Gibbons's assets," he announced before Jared and Mel got comfortable.

"Excuse me?" Mel cocked an eyebrow. "I don't think I understand."

"His assets," Chesterfield barked. "What will happen to the money he's got in the bank?"

"I don't know how to answer that." Mel looked to Jared for insight. "Um ... why are you asking?"

"Because that guy swindled me out of ten thousand dollars when handling my divorce," Chesterfield replied without hesitation. "He told me my ex wouldn't get a dime and I ended up paying a thousand bucks a month in child support. I mean ... does that sound like nothing to you?"

"No, it doesn't." Jared chose his words carefully. "I guess I'm confused. I was under the impression Mr. Gibbons was considered the best divorce attorney in the area."

"Why do you think I hired him?"

"Does that mean he didn't deliver what he promised?"

"Not even close. He told me where to hide my assets – and I followed his instructions to the letter – and I still got nailed with a huge financial settlement. As far as the judge was concerned, I was a pauper. My ex-wife told him I was hiding money, which he couldn't prove, and I still got nailed."

Jared fought the urge to grab the guy by the collar and start shaking. "So ... you're saying that Mr. Gibbons instructed you to illegally hide funds?"

It was only then that Chesterfield realized his mistake. He immediately tried to backtrack. "Oh, well ... ."

"You might want to think about what you say from time to time," Mel suggested. "As for right now, I'm more interested in how many of his clients Gibbons instructed to lie. Did you specifically go to him because you were aware of that tendency?"

"I'm not sure I should answer that." Chesterfield turned prim and adopted a grave look. "I was merely caught off guard when I heard about the passing of my former lawyer and I wanted to make sure that you were dedicated to solving his murder."

"We're definitely dedicated," Jared confirmed. "In fact, since you're so eager to help, it's probably best you tell us where you were between the hours of ten and four last night."

Chesterfield let loose a pained expression. "Oh, geez. Do I have to?"

"Yup."

"What if I ask for a lawyer?"

"That's certainly your prerogative."

"If you have nothing to hide, you don't need a lawyer, though," Mel prodded.

"Fine. I'll tell you. That guy, though, he keeps screwing me. I can't tell you how glad I am that he's dead."

"Believe it or not, that seems to be a popular sentiment."

AFTER SPENDING AN HOUR WITH CHESTERFIELD, Jared and Mel were both convinced he was innocent. That didn't mean they were happy with his attitude and Mel was more than happy to drop a tip to his divorce judge in case there was something that could be done about the missing funds.

After that, they went to Gibbons's office so they could have a sit-down with his law firm's senior partner Stanley Appleman.

"I can't tell you what a shock Carl's murder was to us," Appleman said as he ushered the men to his private office and gestured toward two wingback chairs across from his desk. "I expected you to stop by ... although I had no idea it would be this soon."

"We try not to let murders sit too long," Jared replied. "This one was especially brutal and we're worried that we have a violent killer on the loose."

"I'm guessing Carl's clientele will be included in the suspect pool," Appleman noted, tugging on his suit vest as he sank into his chair. "You should know, we're going to need a warrant to turn over his case files."

"We're well aware of that," Mel confirmed. "The necessary paperwork has been filed and we're waiting for a judge to sign off on it. We'll deliver it to you once we have it."

"Of course. We want to be as helpful as possible."

"That's good," Jared said. "The thing is, believe it or not, we've already had visits from two of his former clients."

"I see."

"Cheryl Wagner directed us toward her ex-husband, who apparently threatened to castrate Carl. Morris Chesterfield stuck his foot in his mouth and outed himself as a suspect."

"I don't doubt that." Appleman rubbed his forehead as he shook his head. "I'm not sure what you want me to say. Even though those clients approached you, I still need the warrant to discuss their cases. We're bound by ethics."

"Oh, we're not here because we want you to talk about Gibbons's clients," Mel intoned. "We're here because we want your insight into the man himself. We've been informed that he was instructing his clients to hide money from the court system and are curious if that's something everyone at this firm does."

"Certainly not." Appleman sat ramrod straight. "We don't condone that sort of thing. Are you certain that Carl was doing that?"

"Yes."

"Well ... if we'd known, he would've been fired. We strictly follow the letter of the law."

He seemed sincere, but Jared had met more than one attorney who could've won an Academy Award in his free time. "What can you tell us about Mr. Gibbons?"

"Well ... he was a shark." Appleman relaxed into his chair. "We added him to the firm because he had a tremendous record when it came to winning cases. That made him a big draw, and he was consistently busy. I would say that eighty percent of his clients were happy with the outcomes of their cases."

"Is that good?" Jared asked blankly.

"That's phenomenal. You have to understand, when you're dealing with divorce cases, things can go off the rails relatively quickly. It's much different than criminal cases, where someone is always guilty of something. Most of the time, when dealing with a contentious divorce, both parties are guilty. The difficult part is trying to figure out the truth, because matters of guilt become a game of degrees."

"I can see that," Mel noted. "Right now, we're interested in Carl the man. We understand he was dating Gloria Harlow. What can you tell us about their relationship?"

Jared internally cringed at the question but managed to hold himself together.

"He brought Gloria to an office party about two weeks ago," Appleman replied. "They started dating after she interviewed us to see if she wanted to switch attorneys. Apparently, instead of doing that, she decided to date Carl. She was a ... peculiar potential client. Her divorce is ... messy."

"We're well aware of her divorce," Mel said. "Trust me. We probably know more about her divorce than you do. I'm more interested in her relationship with Carl. Did you ever see them fight? Was there a reason for her to want to hurt him?"

"Wait." Appleman held up a hand. "Is Gloria a suspect?"

"Gloria is a person of interest."

Jared wanted to sink lower in his chair. Only the need for professionalism kept him rigid.

"Well, I don't know what I can tell you." Appleman changed gears quickly. "She's not a client so there's no reason I can't speak openly about her. The thing is, I honestly can't see her being capable of carrying out a murder. I mean ... you've met the woman, right? She's not the sort who likes to get her hands dirty. Besides that, what would be the point? Murder is either a crime of passion or opportunity. What would Gloria get out of either scenario?"

"They were dating," Mel pointed out.

"Yes, but Carl was a dog who cheated his own ex-wife out of money in their divorce and Gloria was known for keeping a man around for two months at the most before gladly moving on. Carl was bragging about that."

Jared's interest was officially piqued. "Wait ... Carl screwed his own wife in a divorce?"

"Yes, Fran. That was also not our case so I can talk about it. He raked her over the coals. That's how he got his thirst for divorce law and where he cut his teeth. They've been divorced about fifteen years or so and he got out of paying any child support even though they had a minor child."

"How did he manage that?"

"Even I'm not privy to that information." Appleman let loose a hollow chuckle. "Carl was already divorced by the time he joined the firm. He had his own practice back in those days. I only know about it because it was a big deal when everything went down."

"I guess I'm confused," Mel hedged. "Why would the divorce of one attorney be such a big deal?"

"We're all in a circle together. Even if we don't operate out of the same office, we like to gossip about one another. What Carl managed to pull off in his divorce with Fran was nothing short of extraordinary.

"I mean ... she was a stay-at-home mother – at his insistence, mind you – and she had a young boy to take care of," he continued. "All Carl left her with was the home they shared, which was underwater thanks to a bad mortgage. She had to absorb all that debt and he didn't give her a dime."

"Did he hide funds from her?" Jared asked. "I mean ... she should've gotten half of everything in his accounts, right?"

"My understanding is that she didn't get anything. Whether he hid funds or not ... ," Appleman broke off, clearly uncomfortable with the question.

"Listen, we're not idiots," Mel supplied. "It's very clear that Gibbons was an unethical lawyer. All of this is going to come out. It's probably best for you to come clean now so we can tell the reporters who will be asking questions – and the judges, who will probably be interested in what we find out – that you cooperated. Now is not the time to stonewall us."

"I have no intention of stonewalling you. I simply need the warrant. We're in a precarious position for an entirely different reason from what you seem to imagine. I don't want to cut you out of the information. In fact, the sooner you solve this, the better it is for everyone."

"We'll have the warrant soon," Mel promised. "Once we do, we need you to work with us. This is going to get ugly if we're not careful."

"I'm afraid it's probably too late to stop that."

"Then we need to keep it from getting out of hand." Mel was firm. "I'll call the judge's office and see if we can move the paperwork along."

"And I will have a paralegal gather files that will probably be of interest."

"Then we'll go from there."

"That seems to be the best plan."

Seven

Fran Gibbons was a small woman. Jared estimated her height at just over five feet. She had tiny hands and diminutive shoulders ... and she seemed downright surprised to find two police detectives knocking on her door.

"Is this about Carl?" She looked uncertain.

"Yes, ma'am." Jared instantly felt sorry for her. She almost looked afraid to let them into her house, which to his way of thinking suggested emotional abuse. He had no way of proving that, of course, but it was the first thing that jumped into his head.

"Come in." Fran led the men to a tiny living room. The house was a two-story bungalow, probably built in the 1940s, Jared guessed as he looked over the moldings and antiquated light fixtures. The house was tidy but there was very little furniture and almost nothing of value spread about for visitors to "ooh" and "aah" about.

"We don't want to take up much of your time," Jared offered, annoyance at a dead man threatening to take him over. "You obviously heard about Carl's death, though."

"I did," she agreed, gesturing toward the kitchen table. "I'm making tea. I only have chamomile, but if you want some ... ."

"Tea would be lovely," Mel said hurriedly. He was also taken aback by Fran's living conditions. "Did you learn about your ex-husband's death via television?"

"I don't have a television."

That only served to infuriate Jared more. "You have heard about his death, though, right?"

"Yes." Fran removed the teakettle from the stove just as it started to whistle. "One of the neighbors actually told me. I turned on the radio news station so I could hear about it ... although they didn't go into much detail."

"He was discovered during the snowstorm yesterday," Mel explained. "Someone stabbed him multiple times."

"That's awful."

There was very little inflection to the words and Jared didn't have to guess as to how she really felt. "It's okay if you're not sorry he's dead. Quite frankly, we've yet to find anyone who is appalled by his passing."

Fran's expression never shifted. "He's the father of my son. I don't want him dead, no matter what he did."

"Then you're a much better person than him," Jared offered, leaning back in his chair as he regarded the woman. The fabric at the elbows of her cardigan looked as if they were about to give way and her hair was shot through with gray. She was the exact opposite of Gloria, something that Jared couldn't help acknowledging. "We need information about your relationship with Carl."

"I figured as much." Fran's hands were steady as she poured water into mugs. "What do you want to know?"

"How did you end up together in the first place?" Mel asked. "Forgive me for saying, but you don't seem like Carl's type."

"I wasn't always poor and in need of a good dye job." She was rueful as she carried the mugs to the table. "I come from money, if you can believe that. Well ... at least money in this area. I went to the same college as Carl — Rochester University — and we met when I was a sophomore and he was a senior.

"I thought he was ridiculously charismatic and fell for him right away," she continued. "My parents warned me against dating him. They were always strict when it came to boys and I was starting to chafe under their watchful eye. I didn't listen — heck, I didn't want to listen — but it's become glaringly obvious over the years that they were right. That doesn't do me much good now but back then, well, I probably should've listened to them."

Jared was appalled. "Are you not in contact with your family any longer?"

"They wrote me off when I married Carl," she replied. "They warned me it wouldn't end well. They didn't want him included in our family, were embarrassed. My father is an attorney, too, you see. He's a criminal lawyer in Oakland County. He said he recognized Carl as an ambulance-chaser from the start and wanted me to cut ties with him.

"I was infatuated with Carl, though, and thought we could live on love," she continued with a weak laugh. "That turned out to be one of the more naive things I ever believed. Still, I jumped in with both feet.

"Carl insisted that I marry him right away and not finish school," she said. "My father screamed up and down about it, carried on like a spoiled toddler. He wanted me to stay in school, but I thought Carl made sense. I was an idiot back then. If I had to do it over again, I never would've left school. Ah, well."

She broke off and rubbed her forehead as she sat. "I left school. I think Carl thought my father would eventually soften his stance. That's what he wanted. I can see that now, although I was blind back then."

"You mentioned your father was an attorney," Jared prodded. "Did Carl think he would be able to benefit from that relationship?"

"Definitely. My father was one of the most well-regarded attorneys in the tri-county area. Carl kept trying to find ways to ingratiate himself with my father, but it never ended well. My father was mean ... and dismissive ... and he didn't want anything to do with me while I insisted on being married to Carl."

Jared felt sick to his stomach. It was clear Fran had been mistreated by more than one man. "So ... what happened?"

"Pretty much what you would expect." She held her hands palms out and shrugged. "I got pregnant before the ink on my voluntary withdrawal papers was dry. We were married within two months. We had a baby seven months after that. Carl, Jr. I just call him Junior." She smiled at mention of her son. "He's the only good thing that came out of this."

"How long were you married?" Mel asked gently.

"We divorced when Junior was ten."

Jared did the math in his head. "And how old is he now?"

"Twenty-five. He's putting himself through law school ... with a lot of help from my parents, that is. He works hard to supplement what they give him, though. He says he wants to be like my father instead of his."

"Does he know your father well?"

"My father doesn't have much use for me," she answered, choosing her words carefully. "He thinks I was weak when I married Carl. It only got worse when we divorced and he found out how Carl managed to railroad me. He was furious ... at me as much as Carl."

Jared found his fury building. "I'm sorry to hear that. It sounds like you've had it rough all around."

"Oh, I'm fine." Fran forced a smile for Jared's benefit. "I'm the manager of the bakery over at Thirteen Mile and Groesbeck now. I get benefits and a retirement package. I'll have to work until I'm seventy-five, but eventually I'll get there."

"Yeah, well ... it's still unfair," Jared noted. "You didn't do anything wrong and yet you were screwed on every side."

"One might say I earned some of that by not listening to my parents when they warned me about Carl. They saw him for what he was when I didn't."

"They're still your parents. They should've supported you no matter what."

"They didn't see it that way. They did support Junior, though. Once Carl and I were separated, they went out of their way to help Junior. They took him once a week and spent time with him. They saw that he had decent clothes when he was in school. My parents helped pay his college tuition and for law school. They're very good like that."

The information didn't make Jared feel better. "I don't understand why they can't forgive and forget where you're concerned."

"There's too many bad feelings to contend with. It's better this way.

I only care that Junior gets what he needs, and he seems to be ... so that's that."

"Yeah, well ... ." Jared dragged a restless hand through his hair as he regrouped. "It's been explained to us that Carl completely screwed you over in the divorce. He somehow arranged it so he didn't have to pay you a penny, even in child support."

"That's true." Fran swallowed hard. "I wasn't all that upset when Carl said he wanted a divorce. We hadn't been happy for a very long time. In fact, I'm not sure we were ever really happy. I digress, though.

"He announced he wanted a divorce, said he was giving me the house and planned to move out, and that we would meet in a few weeks to discuss how everything would shake out," she continued. "Instead, I was served three days later, found out the house was going to drag me under financially, and the divorce was rammed through six weeks later ... and I didn't get a thing. It was an eye-opening experience."

"But how?" Mel asked. "I can't see a judge simply allowing that to stand. You had a minor child."

"On paper we shared custody and that's all that mattered," Fran explained. "He acted like he was doing me a favor by not seeking full custody of Junior. I have to admit ... I was so terrified that he would take my son that I willingly let him screw me to keep Junior in my life. I believed him when he said a judge would take away Junior because I had no marketable job skills."

Jared was convinced, if Carl wasn't already dead, he would strangle the life out of the diabolical man. "I'm sorry you went through it."

"It's over now."

"What about your son, though?"

"I'm here." A new voice entered the fray and when Jared jerked his eyes to the back of the room, he found a twenty-something man with brown eyes watching him dubiously.

"You're Carl, Jr.?" Mel asked.

"I prefer going by Junior," he said as he moved to the spot behind his mother. His eyes reflected suspicion as he glanced around the room. "May I ask what you gentlemen are doing here?"

"It's okay, Junior," Fran chided. "They're here to talk about your father. They were just asking simple questions."

"It's not okay." Junior was firm as he folded his arms across his chest. "I assume you're looking to pin my father's death on someone and my mother makes an enticing target. Well, let me tell you something, she's innocent and I'm not going to let you railroad her."

"We have no intention of railroading her," Mel reassured the young man. "We simply wanted to hear about your mother's marriage to your father."

"It was an unhappy time," Junior volunteered. "My mother is a saint, though, and works sixty hours a week. She didn't kill my father."

Jared was impressed with Junior's fortitude. Of course, if Fran was his mother, he would've gone overboard standing up for her, too. The woman had been through a terrible ordeal and yet she came out the other side refusing to blame anyone for the things she was forced to overcome. She was a pure soul, something Jared figured out five seconds upon meeting her.

"We're not accusing your mother," Mel promised. "Since she didn't regularly engage with your father, now seems like a weird time for her to finally get her revenge."

"Yes, well ... ." Junior remained suspicious as he grabbed the kettle and poured more hot water into his mother's mug. "If you're not here because she's a suspect, why are you here?"

"We were hoping she might have some information regarding your father's enemies," Mel replied. "It seems he had quite a few of them."

"That was something he took pride in," Junior explained. "He always told me that he wasn't doing his job correctly if he didn't make someone want to kill him."

"That might be a colorful saying, but it creates a problem for us," Jared noted. "We need to find out who hated him enough to kill him."

"I don't know what to tell you." Junior rested his hand on Fran's shoulder. "My mother didn't kill my father. She doesn't have it in her."

"What about your relationship with your father?"

"It was ... fairly normal," Junior replied, tilting his head in consideration. "He wasn't a bad guy where I was concerned. I only saw him one day a month, though. He would take me to the mall and buy me something on the fourth Saturday of each month. He thought that would mean he was my favorite because my mother couldn't afford to buy me anything.

"All that did was make me realize what he truly was," he continued. "I didn't dislike my father. I didn't hate him. He was emotionally limited, though. He wasn't an easy man to get along with. On top of that, my mother was the true parent. She's the one who went to all my parent-teacher conferences.

"She played with me when I was a kid, helped me with my homework, and sat with me when I had a broken heart as a teenager," he continued. "She taught me right from wrong. My father had a more flexible moral code."

"Yes, we've heard about that flexibility," Jared drawled. "Your father was considered a shark in divorce lawyer circles."

"That was a title he happily carted around. In fact, I believe the last set of business cards he purchased said exactly that."

Jared arched an eyebrow. "I see. What about your relationship with your father now? How would you describe it?"

"Boring," Junior replied without hesitation. "I saw him occasionally. I guess it would still be about once a month, but as I got older those visits moved from the mall to a restaurant. He would always pick an expensive one and buy me lunch. It was almost as if he was bragging."

"Did that bother you?" Mel asked.

"Yes. I can't remember when my mother last got to have an expensive meal." Junior's eyes momentarily fired. "I take her out for her birthday every year, but she always selects the cheapest thing on the menu because she doesn't want to be a burden. I hate that my father did that to her."

"And yet you still spent time with him," Jared noted.

"He was my father." For a brief moment, helplessness washed over Junior's features. "I don't know how to explain it. Part of me hated him. No, Mom, I often hated him." He squeezed Fran's hand when she made a move to protest the words. "It's not easy for me to admit, especially since it probably makes me a suspect, but he wasn't easy to deal with."

"He was still your father, though." Jared understood the sentiment.

"You saw him once a month, which probably means you weren't very close. What were those meals like?"

"I basically sat around and listened to him brag about how he screwed people in court," Junior replied. "He got off on it. Winning was more important than money, but the money was really important, too. He couldn't stop himself from bragging. It's simply who he was.

"When you compare that to my grandfather, a man who happens to believe justice is more important than winning, he becomes even more of a louse," he continued. "My grandfather is a jerk in a different way. And, before you think I'm talking bad about him, I've told him that more than once. He thinks it's funny when I stand up to him ... which is exactly why he's still paying for my schooling.

"I plan to pay him back," he said. "I'll make sure he gets every penny. For now, though, I have an uneasy relationship with him. It's for different reasons than why I had an uneasy relationship with my father, though. I respect my grandfather. I tolerated my father."

The young man was soft-spoken and yet blunt. Jared liked that about him. "Did your father ever mention having enemies to you?"

"He bragged about it. He was proud people hated him."

"I guess I'm more interested in him being worried about someone wanting to hurt him," Jared hedged. "Whoever killed your father most likely issued the sort of threats that would cause chills instead of laughter."

"I understand what you're saying." Junior stroked his chin as he thought about it. "He didn't mention anything at our last lunch. That was about two weeks ago. All he talked about at the time was the new woman he was seeing."

A sense of dread weighed down Jared's shoulders. "And what did he say about her?"

"I can't really remember. Um ... her name was Gloria. He said she pretended to be forty-four, but she was really in her fifties. Apparently she was quite ... energetic. That's the word he used to describe her."

"Did you meet her? What about the other women he dated?" Mel asked.

"Oh, I met very few of Dad's dates, although I'm familiar with Gloria's name and fairly certain I've met her at various functions,"

Junior replied. "I might've even met her at a party not too long ago, although I can't be certain. If I did, it was brief.

"I don't particularly remember her offhand," he continued. "As for my father's dates, they were never around long enough for me to even remember most of them. He liked to brag about his sexual conquests, but I once saw he had a Viagra prescription — he pulled it out of his wallet once when trying to boast about all the money he had in there and didn't notice me looking — so I figured those stories were mostly made up."

"That's probably a good presumption," Jared agreed. "The thing is, someone out there hated your father enough to kill him. It's possible that one of his former clients — or more likely the ex-partner of one of his former clients — bided his or her time and then went after him when they thought the coast was clear. It's more likely, though, that he upset someone recently and that's who went after him."

"Are you looking at the girlfriend?"

Jared cleared his throat, uncomfortable. "We're looking at everyone right now. In fact, we're about to pick up a warrant so we can go through your father's case files. We don't have a specific suspect right now. We hope that changes relatively quickly, though."

"I hope so, too," Junior said. "The man was a lousy husband and an absent father, but he was still my dad. I don't want anyone to get away with his murder."

"None of us want that. We'll let you know when we have more information."

"I would appreciate that. Thank you."

Eight

J ared met Harper downtown for dinner. He was surprised by
the text she sent, which basically said "meet me at Jason's
restaurant at seven" and didn't question the reasoning behind
it. He already understood why she did it. Together time with
her parents was obviously wearing on her and she needed an excuse to
be away from them ... and maybe drink.

In fact, she already had a huge martini sitting in front of her when
Jared arrived. She was halfway through it and seemed to be ranting at a
feverish pace as her friend Jason Thurman sat next to her and listened
to the diatribe with sympathetic eyes.

"And then they started arguing about which one of them had worse
taste in partners," Harper said as Jared shrugged out of his coat and
hung it over the back of his chair. "They actually got in a competition
with one another about who has worse taste in dates. Can you believe
that?"

"That sounds ... kind of funny," Jason said after a beat, smiling at
Jared as the police officer leaned over the table to press a kiss to Harper's cheek.

"It wasn't funny." Harper scowled as she flicked her eyes to Jared. "I
blame you for this."

"I'm glad you're pounding the alcohol if you're blaming me." He flashed a worried smile. "Heart, I don't want to be a nag, but do you think you should be drinking hard liquor if you have to drive home?"

"That shows what you know. I didn't drive here. My car is back at the house. My father insisted on driving because he said my mother taught me how to drive — which isn't even true, mind you, because she was always too busy to do it — and he dropped me off downtown when I couldn't take another second of their fighting. I told him I had work at the office and walked from there."

Jared made a face as he slid into his chair. "That's like seven blocks away. You walked that far in this cold?"

"It was better than hanging out with my parents."

"Okay." Jared wasn't sure what response she was looking for so he ran a hand through his hair to brush away the light dusting of snow that had fallen on him between the parking lot and the front door of the restaurant and sipped the glass of water waiting for him. "I take it you didn't have a good day."

Jason held up a hand to still the conversation. "I'm going to warn you that questions regarding her day are going to involve some really loud answers. She's been here for forty-five minutes and barely taken a breath. All I asked is how things were going."

"I see," Jared smirked at the gregarious restaurant owner. When Jason first arrived in town, he had designs on Harper. They briefly dated in high school before he was forced to move away. He hoped they would have a second chance, but his hopes were quickly dashed when he saw Harper and Jared together. Now he was merely a friend to them, although he still irritated Jared from time to time. That was on purpose. "I'm betting you were willing to listen to the diatribe, huh?"

"While feeding her martinis." Jason winked. "By the way, I noticed the ring on her finger. I guess you finally got it together and proposed, huh? Congratulations."

Jared's smile widened. "It was a Christmas gift of sorts."

"For both of us," Harper added, finishing her drink. "I think I need another one."

Jason moved to stand, as if he was going to get the drink for her, but Jared shook his head, confusing the bartender who could do nothing but lift an eyebrow. "No?"

"I think you should have some food before you have another drink, Heart," Jared admonished. "I don't happen to believe that drinking when you're this worked up is a good thing."

"Why?" Her expression was blank. "I'm not driving."

"No, but I would like to talk to you, have a nice dinner conversation, and I don't think the liquor is going to make that possible."

Instead of arguing, Harper let loose a world-weary sigh that made Jason snort. "Fine. I'm done drinking." She pushed the empty glass toward Jason. "I want a Shirley Temple. If I can't have the liquor, I'll get hopped up on sugar instead."

"Now you're talking." Jared leaned back in his chair and kicked out his long legs in front of him. "Tell me about your day."

"You're stepping in it now." Jason carefully backed away from the table. "I think I'll get your drinks and let you guys talk about this in private ... because you're engaged now and that seems like the respectful thing to do."

Jared glowered at him and shook his head. "I'll have an iced tea. Thank you."

"You're welcome." Jason clapped him on the shoulder and leaned close so he could whisper. "Don't ask about what happened when she took her parents to the coffee shop. It's best left forgotten."

Jared's lips twitched, but he remained calm as he held Harper's gaze. "Tell me about your day," he repeated. "I'm sorry I wasn't in touch, but I had a lot going on. We conducted quite a few interviews and then the entire afternoon was spent going through Gibbons's client files."

Harper fixed him with a dark stare. "What did Jason just say to you?"

"That he was going to get our drinks."

"He said more than that."

"He said I was a lucky man because I'm marrying you. I happen to agree with that."

Harper rolled her eyes so hard it was a miracle she didn't fall out of her chair. "He said something else. I know the way his mind operates. He's a snarky guy and he's been listening to me for a long time."

"I can't remember what he said."

"Liar!"

Jared extended a warning finger. "Please don't make a scene. This is your friend's restaurant. You shouldn't talk so loudly in it that you scare away his customers."

The admonishment hit hard and Harper's face crumbled. "I'm sorry." She meant it. "I don't mean to rant and rave like this. It's just ... my parents. You have no idea how annoying my parents are. I feel as if I'm caught in high school again.

"Those years stuck under that roof with them when I was old enough to understand what was going on were the worst in my life," she continued. "I mean ... it was painful. I didn't understand why they stayed together. They obviously hated each other to the point where they couldn't stand to look at one another."

Jared's heart went out to her. "I'm sorry. I don't know what that's like. My parents always got along. And, when they didn't, they took fights behind closed doors. Those times were rare, though."

"You're lucky." Harper leaned her forehead on her hand and rubbed. "We found Carl's ghost, by the way. He was hanging around outside the house."

Jared glanced around to make sure nobody had heard her — he was still leery when she openly talked about her gifts — but absolutely no one was looking in their direction. "Did he say anything?"

"He didn't even realize he was dead. It's going to take some time for him to remember. He was much more interested in picking a fight with Mom ... who couldn't even see him."

"He wanted to fight with your mother?" Jared didn't like the sound of that. "How come?"

"That's a very good question. I have no idea why. He seemed most upset because my father was with us. He called my mother a charlatan, which might've been funny if my head wasn't already pounding thanks to the arguments."

"I'm sorry." Jared had no idea how to make her feel better. "Maybe you shouldn't spend time with your parents."

"Why do you think I didn't move back in with them after college? I could have. It would've saved me money. The idea made me want to throw something through a window, though."

"Your mother?"

Harper's lips curved. "There are times I would definitely like to throw her through a window."

"I don't know what to tell you, though. You either have to cut them out of your life or put your foot down. I don't expect the former and I've never seen you do the latter."

Harper balked. "I put my foot down."

"When?"

"When ... ." She trailed off, uncertain. "I'll come up with an instance. Just you wait. Until then, tell me about your day."

Since she seemed to need the distraction, Jared did just that. He launched into a long tale that encompassed all his interviews, and when he was finished, Harper was intent.

"It sounds to me like Carl was a real jerk," she said as she ate the salad that had been delivered between stories. "I figured that out myself because he was trying to hit on me and asked if ghosts can have sex."

Jared made a face. "That is lovely. Wait ... can they?"

"Why are you asking?"

"Because, if it's possible, we could both decide to stay behind as ghosts and keep things exactly how we like them. That would be years and years from now, mind you, but it's nice to have options."

Despite herself, Harper smiled. "That's kind of cute ... but we don't want to do that. We'll just go to the other side together. I don't know what's over there — I've only seen glimpses, after all — but I think it will be a fabulous place to spend our happily ever after."

Jared caught her hand and brought it to his lips. "I don't care where we end up as long as we're together."

"That's sweet." She was much more relaxed than she had been when he first sat down. "I'm sorry about being a ranting monster earlier. I just can't seem to help it. They drive me crazy."

"I think it's a parent's job to drive their child crazy."

"Your mother doesn't drive you crazy."

"No, but ... it's different. Your parents are wired differently than mine were. Frankly, I think it's a miracle that you turned out semi-sane. You could've been a real basket case."

"I'm not too far from there right now."

"You're fine." He kissed her palm and released her hand. "I don't want to dwell on your mother, but she went to her own house, right? She's not still hanging around our house, is she?"

"Not if she knows what's good for her." Harper's gaze momentarily darkened. "I left her with my father. They were fighting about whether or not he liked cream in his coffee. I had to get away from them so I walked from the coffee shop to the office. It wasn't any more comfortable there because Eric and Molly were making out like high schoolers on the couch but even that was preferable to listening to my parents."

Eric Tyler and Molly Parker were Harper's employees at GHI, Ghost Hunters, Inc. Harper and Zander started the business after college, not caring if they were the laughingstock of the community, because it seemed wise to take advantage of Harper's peculiar gift. They'd made a real go of it and most people didn't even question what they did for a living. There were some, of course, who looked down on them, but Harper wasn't the type to dwell on that.

"They're in love," Jared teased. "I would much rather have him making out with her rather than mooning after you."

"He did that for like five minutes."

"I'm betting he did that quite frequently before we started dating, but it doesn't matter. They're together and happy. I take it there are no new clients."

"Believe it or not, the run-up to Christmas and the few weeks right after is a slow time for us."

"Ghosts respect the holidays?"

"No, people just decide they would rather put up with ghosts until all their shopping is complete. January is a dead zone because most everybody is in debt. Things will pick up nicely in February."

"Thanks for the tip."

"I don't mind the lull right now," she admitted. "What I can't stand is that the one case we do have involves my mother. She doesn't even seem to be a little sorry that he's dead."

Jared wanted to quiz her regarding Gloria's reaction but it felt invasive ... especially given his motivations. He wasn't ready to tell Harper her mother was a legitimate suspect in their murder investigation. His heart hurt at the mere thought.

"Well, if your mother is no longer dwelling with us — and I can't tell you how excited that makes me — I have a suggestion," he offered, his eyes twinkling. "How about we finish dinner, pick up some cake and ice cream from the bakery, head home and eat it naked in front of the fireplace?"

Harper chuckled. "You had that one ready to just whip out, didn't you?"

He nodded. "Ever since I saw that fireplace."

"I think it sounds like a fantastic idea." She spoke from the heart. "A few hours of just the two of us is exactly what the doctor ordered."

"Good. I'm sorry your day didn't go well."

"I am, too. My night is looking up, though."

"You've got that right."

HARPER WAS COMPLETELY SOBER and back to her normal self when she and Jared landed at the house. She carried the bag with the cake and ice cream while he gave chase, and they were breathless when they made it inside.

"I really do love you," Harper murmured as Jared helped her out of her coat, his mouth on hers.

He laughed at the muffled words. He understood them completely. "I really love you, too. You have no idea how much."

"Oh, I think I do." She held onto his arm as she kicked off her boots and dragged him toward the living room. "Come on. I'm starving for cake ... and you."

"That makes two of us."

Jared flicked the switch on the gas fireplace to turn it on and then frowned when he heard a noise from the other end of the house.

Harper, apparently oblivious, sat cross-legged on the floor. "Come on. I'll feed you cake."

"Just a second, Heart." Jared craned his neck to look down the hallway that led to the guest bedroom. "Did you hear that?"

"All I hear is my own pounding heart." Harper opened the container that held the chocolate cake. "Do you think it's wrong of me to want to rub this frosting all over your chest and lick it off?"

Jared caught her hand as she reached for his belt loop and gave her a curt shake of his head. Finally catching up to his mood, she frowned.

"Is something wrong?"

"I think someone is in the house." Jared hated uttering the words because all the playfulness vacated Harper's face in two seconds flat. "I need you to put your boots on and get ready to run across the road in case I find something." He drew his service weapon and held up his hand to still her when she opened her mouth to argue. "Do it."

Her heart rate picked up a notch as she slowly got to her feet and trudged toward the front door. She felt as if the weight of the world was resting on her shoulders as she tugged on the boots and watched Jared slip into the hallway. He didn't call out to her, whisper words of reassurance or love as he readied himself to face an enemy. He was too intent on hunting whoever was stupid enough to break into a cop's house.

Harper knew she should've stayed in the foyer and prepared herself to flee, but she couldn't swallow the idea of leaving Jared to fight with a potential intruder on his own. Instead, she cut toward the hallway and scampered behind him, ignoring the dirty look he shot her when she caught up.

He gestured in the opposite direction, his expression serious. She shook her head.

"Go," he whispered.

"No." She refused to back down. "We're doing this together."

"There's no *we*. I'm the cop. I'm the one who is armed." He kept his voice low.

"There's always a *we*. I'm going with you. The longer we stand here arguing about it, the more time we waste. It might be nothing. Maybe my mother left the fan on in the room or something."

Jared arched an eyebrow. He hadn't even considered that. "That fan is old."

"Yeah, and it creaks ... just like that noise I heard a second ago. There's probably no one in the house." She hoped that was true.

"You stay behind me just in case."

"I will. I'm not leaving you, though. You wouldn't leave me."

"Those are entirely different circumstances, but we'll argue about it later." Jared squeezed her hand and then reached for the door handle. "Get ready."

She nodded and stared at the door, willing the room to be empty so she and Jared could go back to their romantic evening.

Jared sucked in a breath and shoved open the door, frowning when he saw a hint of movement and heard a theatrical gasp.

"Who is that?" a voice bellowed.

Harper frowned. "Mom?"

Annoyed, Jared felt along the wall until he found the light switch and flicked it. When the room was bathed in light, he almost fell over. Gloria wasn't alone.

Harper was horrified. "Dad?"

The bickering Harlows were doing a different kind of fighting tonight. It was the sort that necessitated dueling tongues and nudity.

"Shut off the light!" Gloria barked. "We're having a private moment, for crying out loud. What are you even thinking?"

Harper was convinced she was going to pass out. "Oh, my ... they're naked."

"I see that." Jared was flummoxed. "I feel sick."

"You're not the only one."

Nine

"I think I've lost the ability to hear." Harper jerked her head back and forth to make the muffling effect closing in over her dissipate. "Or maybe ... ." She listed to the side.

Jared caught her before she hit the floor. She didn't pass out. Her legs simply went out as she struggled to come to grips with what she was seeing.

"Harper!" He drew her to him and pressed a hand to her pale face. "Stay with me," he ordered.

"I'm with you. I'm just having a terrible nightmare."

"If you are, we're sharing it." He clutched her to his chest and glared at Gloria and Phil, who had the good sense to draw the blankets up to their chests and cover themselves. "What are you doing?"

"What do you mean?" Gloria's face was a mask of innocence. "We're not doing anything. What are you doing?"

"You can't be serious."

"Oh, I'm serious." She was more comfortable going on the offensive, so that's exactly what she did. "Have you ever heard of knocking?"

Jared wanted to smother her with the pillow Phil had surreptitiously moved on top of his lap. Even though he was covered with blankets, there was obviously a lot going on underneath them. "This is my house," he reminded her. "Besides, we didn't think you were spending the night."

Gloria made a sad sniffling noise. "Of course I'm spending the night. I'm in mourning. My boyfriend was just murdered. It's a trying time for me."

"Uh-huh." Jared smoothed the back of Harper's hair as she buried her face in his neck. Obviously seeing her parents together was too much for her. Frankly, it was too much for him, too. "It's so trying you're having sex with your ex-husband in your daughter's house."

She was blasé. "We were just blowing off steam. It's not a big deal."

"Not a big deal? You guys have been mired in the most contentious divorce in the history of divorces since I met you."

"So what?"

"It's not what you think," Phil offered, speaking for the first time. His cheeks were as red as Santa's pants. "Gloria was upset and needed some sympathy. I was upset on her behalf — I mean, some people think she's a murderer, for crying out loud — and one thing just led to another. It's not a big deal. It happens all the time."

Harper turned her face from Jared's neck and focused on her father. "What do you mean? How does it happen all the time?"

"It just does." Phil grinned broadly. "We tend to do this at least once a month, sometimes even twice. It's honestly not a big thing. There's nothing to worry about."

"See." Gloria held up her hand. "If you guys would've knocked, we wouldn't even be having this discussion. We would already be finished. Now we're going to have to start all over again."

"Oh, my ... ." Harper couldn't find the correct words to express how she was feeling.

The only words Jared could find were of the cursing variety. "We're going to bed," he gritted out. "I want this — whatever this is — to be over. I don't want to hear another sound from this room. Do you understand?"

"Oh, geez." Gloria rolled her eyes. "You don't have to be such a spoilsport. You've been having sex with our daughter for almost a year now and you don't hear us complaining. In fact, that's the one aspect of your relationship I encourage. The rest of it is kind of ... meh."

Jared huffed out a series of unintelligible syllables that didn't form words.

"It's fine," Phil supplied. "There really is nothing to worry about. You guys go to bed. We'll just finish up and you'll never know we were here."

"I think I might be having an aneurysm," Harper muttered against Jared's ear.

"You're not the only one, Heart. Come on. We're taking the cake and ice cream and locking ourselves in the bedroom. As for you two ... ." He openly glared at his future in-laws. "I don't want to hear a sound from this room for the rest of the night. Do you understand me?"

Phil dutifully nodded, but Gloria was having none of it.

"If there's no noise then you're not doing it right. Would you like me to go into detail for you? I have a book at home. It's for women over forty — I got it four years ago — but it might do you some good."

"Not one sound," Jared hissed. "I just ... you guys are absolutely sickening. I can't believe you!"

HARPER WOKE IN THE USUAL position. She was curled in at Jared's side, her head resting on his chest. The sun was shining through the window. It was winter, so the birds weren't chirping, but the pedestal fan was whirring next to the bed.

She was warm. She felt loved and safe. And then she remembered the night before.

"Oh, son of a goat sniffer." She rolled away from Jared and buried her head under the covers as he stretched and watched her with trepidation.

"Do you know a lot of goat sniffers, Heart?"

"I thought maybe the world would've ended during the night." Her voice was muffled under the covers. "Apparently we didn't get that lucky."

He chuckled as he reached for the blanket and drew it away from her face. "We're both still in this world. That makes me pretty happy."

Her sea blue eyes were as wide as saucers. "Don't you remember what happened last night?"

"I do and it was jarring."

"It was worse than jarring." She tossed off the covers and sat. Her hair was wild, standing on end, and there was makeup smeared underneath her eyes. She'd forgotten to wash her face before bed because of the horrible ordeal, which was the exact opposite of her normal routine. "It was ... apocalyptic. No, it was worse than that. It was ... tsunami-lyptic. Wait ... is that a word?"

"I don't believe so." He was calm as he combed his fingers through her hair. "It's okay. It's not the end of the world."

Harper's expression was dour. "How can you say that? You saw them. They were ... naked. They were making noises. Oh, man. That noise we thought was the fan was them. What do you think they were doing?"

"I believe we know what they were doing."

"But ... why?" Harper knew she sounded whiny, but she couldn't stop herself. "Do you think they're trying to kill me? I often thought that when I was a kid. I thought they fought because they wanted me to die of embarrassment. Now I think they've switched up their tactics."

"Oh, I don't think it's that bad."

"Of course you don't. You didn't have to see your parents having sex."

"Technically we only heard them having sex. They moved apart pretty quickly when I turned on the light. We didn't see anything."

Harper's glare was withering. "Is that supposed to make me feel better?"

"I have no idea. Did it?"

"No."

"Then it wasn't supposed to make you feel better." His grin was amiable as he regarded her suspicious features. "Oh, Harper, there's no reason to freak out. They're adults ... and they're married. Technically. Your mother says she's forty-four, but she's probably too old to get pregnant so you don't have to worry about that. That's the biggest concern, right?"

Harper's mouth dropped open. "Oh, my ... ."

Jared roared with laughter as he covered her mouth with his. "Do you have any idea how much I love you?"

AN HOUR LATER, AFTER SHOWERING and dressing for the day, Harper and Jared made their way into the kitchen. Gloria and Phil were already up and toiling behind the kitchen island. They looked to be making breakfast and they boasted extremely different expressions when the party widened to four.

"Hello, honey." Phil beamed at his daughter and shuffled around the counter so he could give her a hug. "How are you feeling?"

"Like I want to kill both of you," Harper replied without hesitation. "Don't touch me with those hands. I have no idea where they've been and if you've washed them."

"Oh, I totally washed them."

Harper narrowed her eyes to dangerous slits. "Thank you for that bit of ... relief."

"You're welcome." Phil shot a sidelong look toward Jared before rushing back to hide behind his estranged wife. "We're making pancakes and sausage."

"How awesome," Jared enthused, moving his hand to Harper's back. "I love pancakes."

"Mom loves sausage," Harper offered, pinning her mother with a belligerent look. "Don't you, Mom?"

"I prefer bacon," Gloria said dryly. "I can deal with sausage, though. It has a specific flavor that I adore."

"Ugh." Harper slapped her hand to her forehead. "I know I started it, but I'm going to end it, too. Don't ever talk about sausage in front of me again."

Even though he knew it was a painful situation for Harper, Jared had to bite the inside of his cheek to keep from laughing. "Let's sit at the table," he suggested, prodding Harper in that direction. "I think it's time we had a discussion."

"And I think it's time we didn't." Gloria was firm as she stared down Harper. "This isn't a big deal. In fact, I don't see why you're getting so worked up about it. It's not as if it's the first time we've consoled one another."

"So you mentioned last night." Harper's affect was dull. "I honestly can't believe you guys have been hopping in and out of bed together this entire time. I don't understand it. If you love each other, why are you getting divorced?"

"Because your father is an idiot."

"Because your mother is insufferable."

The answers only served to fire Harper up more. "If you feel that way about each other, why have sex?"

"Oh, well, your father is gifted in that department," Gloria explained. "If I could just get the sex and never have to deal with his mouth ... and the fact that he refuses to pick up his clothes and put them in the hamper ... I would stay married to him forever. Unfortunately, that's not the case."

Harper turned a set of morose eyes to Jared. "This is supposed to be a happy time for us. We're planning a wedding. We have a new house. How could everything that was going so right go so wrong?"

"Oh, my poor Heart." He kissed her forehead. "We'll get it all back ... just as soon as you tell your mother she can't stay here any longer."

"I didn't tell her she could stay here last night."

"You most certainly did," Gloria fired back. "I'm in crisis. I can't stay alone. My boyfriend is dead. That's too much for me to deal with."

"Then go to Dad's house," Harper exploded. "He can comfort you there."

"That won't work. I hate his new house. He won't pick up his things. You know what a pig he is."

Harper buried her head in her arms on the tabletop. "Why me?"

Jared could do nothing but rub her back. "It's going to be fine," he reassured her for what felt like the hundredth time. "We still have each other."

"There is that."

JARED LEFT HARPER TO DEAL with her parents. He had a belly full of pancakes and sausage and a fun story to tell his partner. In fact, when he was finished, Mel was laughing so hard he had to wipe tears from the corners of his eyes.

"Are you serious?"

"Unfortunately, yes."

"I can't believe Phil and Gloria have been doing ... that ... since they separated. I guess it makes sense. They were together a long time and I always wondered what kept them from divorcing years before. That is ... unbelievable, though."

"Harper is a wreck."

"I don't blame her."

"It does make me feel a little better about Gloria, oddly enough."

Mel slid his partner a curious look. "What do you mean? Why would it make you feel better about her?"

"Carl was stabbed five times. That's what the initial autopsy report said. I went over it last night once Harper fell asleep."

"So?"

"So, that kind of overkill usually means it's a crime of passion," Jared replied. "I'm not sure Gloria was passionate about Carl. In fact, given the way she's acting, I'm starting to wonder if she even cares."

"That points to a sociopath," Mel noted. "That doesn't make me feel better about her."

"She's not a sociopath." Jared was almost positive that was true. "She's just a difficult woman. She's selfish and self-centered. She cares more about herself than anyone else. I mean ... how can you have a great kid like Harper and not want to embrace everything about her?"

Mel snorted, genuinely amused. "I think you might be asking that question from a place of bias." He parked in front of Carl's home and killed the cruiser's engine. "I happen to be fond of Harper, too, but she's not exactly what I would call an easy individual."

Jared was instantly on edge. "What is that supposed to mean?"

"Not what you think it does, so simmer down." Mel was stern. "It's just ... think about it from Gloria's perspective. Harper was an only child who started spouting on and on about seeing ghosts when she was a kid. That couldn't have been easy. I know for a fact Gloria thought she was going to have to be institutionalized at some point."

Jared's blood ran cold. "What? Why?"

"You know why. They thought she had mental problems."

"Well, she doesn't."

"And that's all well and good. She's proven herself over and over again since that time. Still, it was weird when it first started happening. The only one who believed her straight off the bat was Zander, and he's got his own issues."

Uncomfortable with the direction of the conversation, Jared shifted so he could look out the window. "What are we doing back here?"

"Talking to Margie Driskell," Mel replied, thankful to be able to change the subject. "She called and left a message. She lives next door and swears she heard Carl fighting with someone the night before he was killed. We now know he died well after midnight, closer to two. The fight was around eight the previous evening. She might make a compelling witness."

"Fine." Jared threw up his hands in defeat. "Let's talk to Margie. Just for the record, though, Harper is wonderful."

"I know."

"She's a dream."

"I know."

"She's the best woman in the world."

Mel bit back a sigh. "I know."

MARGIE WAS FULL OF EXCITEMENT when she let Mel and Jared into her house. She had cookies on the table and fresh tea in mugs so they would have refreshments for the talk. She was in her seventies and lived alone, so she was always open to guests.

"I'm glad you were prompt," she told Mel as she handed him a napkin. "I don't like waiting around with nothing to do and there's a euchre tournament at the senior center this afternoon I don't want to miss."

"Once you called I got over here as quickly as possible," he soothed. "I understand you saw something the night Carl died."

"Well, it's more like I heard it," Margie corrected. "I didn't see much of anything because it gets dark so early these days because of the time of year. I hate that."

"It's definitely a downer," Mel agreed. "What did you hear?"

"Well, Carl was arguing something fierce with someone. I couldn't make out what he was saying, but I could hear raised voices. Whoever was in there with him was giving as good as she got."

Mel arched an eyebrow. "*She?*"

"Yeah. It was a woman. I'm pretty sure it was Gloria Harlow."

Jared's heart sank. "What makes you think it was Gloria?"

"Well, it was her car parked in front of his house – she's got that pair of lips on her back window so you can't miss that it's her – and I saw her through the window."

Mel ran his tongue over his teeth. "Which window?"

"That one." Margie pointed to the one on the other side of the room and Mel slowly got to his feet and strode in that direction so he could look through it.

"This looks almost directly into Carl's living room," he noted.

"Yeah. He's in there all the time. Or, I guess he was. He's not in there now or anything, although you obviously know that because he's dead."

"And you say he and Gloria were fighting?"

"Oh, they were spitting mad. Gloria even threw a pillow at him. Like I said, I couldn't hear what they were saying, but it's obvious they weren't getting along."

Jared swallowed hard when Mel's gaze latched with his. "That doesn't necessarily mean anything. The argument happened hours before he died." He was plaintive when he turned to Margie. "Did you see Gloria drive away?"

"I did." Margie bobbed her head. "She drove away and then came back the next day. I thought everything was fine, that they made up. She was in there a long time. Then, like an hour later, I saw you show up. I realized then that not everything was fine."

"An hour later?" Mel's eyebrows hopped. "That's not good."

Jared felt the ground giving way beneath him. "That still doesn't mean anything."

"Yes, it does." Mel planted his hands on his hips. "It means we're officially bringing Gloria in for questioning. There's no getting around that now."

In his head, Jared knew that was true. His heart still wanted to put up a fight. He couldn't, though. He had a job to do.

"I'll find out where she is." Jared was morose. "This is going to hurt Harper."

"I'm sorry about that. It has to be done. We can't let it go a second longer."

Ten

For lack of anything better to do, Harper decided to escape to the GHI office. She was more interested in watching Molly and Eric make out than she was in dealing with her parents. Unfortunately for her, Gloria and Phil decided to tag along.

"This really isn't necessary," Harper grumbled as she scuffed her feet along the sidewalk in front of the business's front window. "You guys can go do ... whatever it is you do when I'm not around."

"Oh, don't be a sourpuss," Gloria admonished. "We want to spend time with you."

"Why?"

"Because we're your parents."

"You've been my parents since the start," Harper pointed out. "This is the first time you guys have ever wanted to come to work with me."

"That's not true." Phil adjusted his coat to hold off the bracing cold. "I've wanted to join your outings for some time. You always said it wasn't a good idea because it wasn't safe."

Oddly enough, Harper vaguely remembered that conversation. She'd been tickled when her father suggested going on an outing. She'd also been terrified because Phil was the sort of person who needed constant attention. "We're not doing anything but paperwork," she supplied. "You'll be bored."

"Nonsense." Gloria adopted the sternest face in her repertoire. "We're your parents. We want to watch you in action."

"Well ... great." Harper was glum as she strolled through the front door. She barely paid any of her co-workers any notice, including Zander, who was sitting at his desk having a chat with Eric. They both looked toward the people with Harper and the gobsmacked expression on Zander's face was one for the record books.

"Hey, Harp," he called out. "I didn't know you were coming in today."

"That makes two of us." Harper shrugged out of her coat. "I thought it might be a good idea to get ahead on the paperwork and my parents thought it would be a good idea to come with me."

"Oh, your parents." Eric smiled brightly. "I've heard a lot about you Mr. and Mrs. Harlow. Although, to be fair, everything I've heard about you would seem to suggest it's not good for you to be in the same location together."

"We're going through a family ordeal," Phil explained. "We thought it best to do it as a unit."

"*They* thought it best," Harper stressed.

"Harper is in a bad mood," Gloria volunteered. "I expect you to get her out of it, Zander."

"Of course." Zander amiably bobbed his head. He was used to dealing with Gloria and knew exactly how to handle her. "I'll get right on that."

"You do that." Gloria planted her hands on her hips and glanced around the office. "This place needs a spruce. It's far too drab given what you guys do for a living. You need brighter paint ... and maybe a mural."

"A mural?" Eric cocked an eyebrow and looked to Zander for answers. He was clearly confused. "Why would we need a mural?"

"Because it's a proven fact that businesses with murals are more popular than those without murals."

"And what would the mural be of?" Zander queried.

"I don't know." Gloria made an annoyed face. "How about ghosts?

You could do a *Scooby-Doo* mural. That's what I've always pictured when it comes to thinking about you and Harper on a job together."

Zander's lips curved. "I often think that myself."

"Don't encourage her," Harper hissed, shaking her head as she sank into her desk chair. "What's going on here? Do we need to fill out invoices or anything?"

"We're all caught up," Zander replied with a bit of trepidation. It was obvious Harper needed a distraction and he had nothing to give her. "You really didn't need to come in. Things aren't going to pick up until February. It's always like this around the new year."

"I didn't have a choice," Harper growled.

"I don't understand," Eric hedged, shifting so he could lean his hip against the corner of Zander's desk. "Why are you all together?"

"Because Gloria is a suspect in a murder," Phil replied. "That means we're basically at Defcon One."

"You're the only one who says things like that," Gloria shot back. "And I'm not a murder suspect. I was simply dating a dead man. Besides, that's not why we're here. We're here because Harper is going through something existential, a crisis of sorts. As her parents, it's our job to see her through it."

Amusement glinted in the depths of Zander's eyes. "Are you having a crisis, Harp?"

"You have no idea." She rubbed the tender spot between her eyebrows. "I should've stayed in bed and never gotten up today."

"What's wrong?"

"Don't worry about it."

The quick shutdown only made Zander more curious. "What happened?" He turned his gaze to Phil and Gloria. "What did you do to my Harper?"

"We didn't do anything to her," Gloria replied. "She's simply being ridiculous and Phil and I have decided to shadow her until she gets over herself."

"That was actually Gloria's idea," Phil countered. "I thought we should hide and pretend it didn't happen. Eventually Harper will start talking to us again when she's over the shock."

"The shock of what?" Eric asked.

"Don't answer that question," Harper warned, extending a finger in her mother's direction. "I don't want news of this spreading. Nothing good can come of it."

"Oh, pipe down." Gloria rolled her eyes. "Last night, through no fault of our own, Harper walked in on a private moment between her father and me. If she would've knocked, none of this would've happened."

Harper was beside herself. "Through no fault of your own?"

"The door was closed."

"It's my house!" Harper's voice boomed throughout the room. "You were having sex in my house. How is that not my business?"

Zander was convinced he was going to have to pick his jaw up from the ground. "No way."

"They say they do it all the time," Harper added. "Can you believe that? All this time, when they've been fighting about spoons and the velvet Elvis painting, they've secretly been doing it."

"That is ... awesome," Zander said finally. "I can't believe you guys managed to keep that a secret."

"It's not awesome!" Harper wanted to punch someone and Zander made an appealing target. "It's disgusting."

"I don't know about that, Harper." Eric adopted a pragmatic tone. "I mean ... they are your parents. They've obviously had sex before. You wouldn't be here if they hadn't so it's not really disgusting."

"Do you want to be fired?" Harper challenged.

Eric visibly shrank in the face of her fury. "Of course not. Your parents are heathens. I don't know what I was thinking."

"Thank you." Her eyes were on fire when she focused on her mother. "I can't believe you're actually telling people about this. I mean ... have you no shame?"

"Not where this is concerned." Gloria was bland. "It's not a big deal. We're still married so it's not even weird."

"Oh, geez." Harper buried her face in her arms on her desk. "Where are the locusts when I really need them?" She didn't look up when the bell over the door jangled. "I need a bag for my head so I can walk around town without feeling the judgment of others."

When no one immediately responded to her dramatic outburst,

she lifted her head and found Jared and Mel standing in the doorway. Mel looked stern. Jared, well, he looked as if he wanted to be anywhere else.

"What's going on?" Zander asked, immediately picking up on a bad vibe. "Has something happened?"

"It has," Mel confirmed, leveling his gaze on Gloria. "We need to take you in for formal questioning in the death of Carl Gibbons. I'm sorry but ... we don't have a choice."

Harper almost knocked over her chair in her haste to stand. "What do you mean? Why?"

"Heart ... ." Jared looked pained as he took a step in her direction. Mel extended a hand to stop his partner from crossing to her.

"We don't have a choice, Harper," Mel intoned. "Some new information has come to light."

"What information?" Gloria barked. "There is no information because I'm innocent."

Harper swallowed hard. "This can't be right."

Jared wanted to go to her, take her in his arms, soothe the horror that was washing over her features. All he could do was stand to the side and hold out his hands.

"I'm sorry. We have to take her in."

"YOU NEED TO CALM DOWN."

Zander watched Harper pace the lobby of the police station an hour later, a ball of worry pooling in the pit of his stomach. He wanted to help her, ease her distress. He had no idea how to do it.

"You need to calm down," Harper fired back. "It's not your mother that was just arrested by your fiancé."

"She wasn't technically arrested. They're just questioning her."

Harper narrowed her eyes to dangerous slits. "Really? Is that the hill you want to die on?"

"I would rather not die on any hill." Zander refused to back down in the face of her rage. "Harper, they had no choice. You heard them."

"Oh, I heard them." Her tone was dark when she turned her eyes to the interrogation room. It was really a conference room with a big window and her agitation was on full display as she stared through the soundproof glass. "In fact ... ." She took everyone by surprise when she strode toward the door.

"What are you doing?" Zander asked, frustrated.

"I'm going in." Harper's face looked as if it was carved out of granite when she walked into the room. "Hello, gentlemen."

"What are you doing?" Gloria asked as she rubbed her forehead. Phil insisted on staying with her and serving as her representative even though he had no legal standing to do so. "You should stay in the lobby, Harper."

"No." Harper folded her arms over her chest as she plunked down in the chair on her mother's left side and glared at Jared and Mel. "Well, let's have it."

"Harper, you can't be in here," Mel chided. "It's not allowed."

"My father is in here."

"Yes, but ... he won't leave."

"Well, I won't leave either." Harper lifted her chin, defiant. "If you want me out of here, you're going to have to physically remove me."

Mel slid his eyes to Jared, who immediately started shaking his head.

"Don't even think about asking me to do that," Jared warned, his tone low and full of warning. "I will melt down if you do that."

"Fine." Mel held up his hands in defeat. "This is already a circus. Why not make it worse?"

"That's my philosophy," Phil offered helpfully, earning a glare from Mel.

"Gloria, Carl's neighbor says that you were at his house the day before he died," Mel started. "She says there was an argument and you actually threw something at Carl. What do you have to say to that?"

"You're obviously talking about Margie Driskell," she said dryly. "That woman is blind and deaf. There's no way she could identify me from a full house away."

"And yet she did."

"Well ... she's crazy."

"That's not really up for debate," Mel noted. "I need to know if you were at Carl's house."

Gloria heaved out a sigh, the sound long and drawn out. "Yes. I was there. We had a fight. Is that what you want to hear?"

Jared, who had been trying to catch Harper's eye from across the table, felt a sinking sensation in his stomach. "That's not really what we want to hear, Gloria," he replied. "What were you fighting about?"

"Oh, who can say?" She was airy as she fanned herself. "Is it just me or is it hot in here?"

"It's just you," Harper snapped. "Why didn't you tell us about your fight with Carl before this?"

"You know why." Gloria glared at her only daughter. "I knew your boyfriend would suspect me of being a murderer. This is exactly what he's always wanted. He'll be able to get me out of your life and take up residence as the most important person in your orbit if he manages to get the charges to stick."

Harper growled as she rubbed her forehead. "He's already the most important person in my orbit. It's not as if he has to supplant you."

"Ahem!" Zander, who had managed to hear the conversation through the walls (even though that was supposed to be impossible), banged on the window to get his best friend's attention. "I'm the most important." He thumped his chest. "That's never going to change."

"Oh, geez." Mel glared at his nephew. "Why don't we invite the entire town to this interview? I mean ... everybody is practically in here now as it is."

Jared ignored him and focused on Gloria. "I don't want you in prison. Harper would end up hurt in that scenario and that's the last thing I want. How can you not recognize that?"

"Because you've always hated me," she responded without hesitation. "I see the way you look at me. You think I'm silly and vapid. I'm not oblivious."

"I think you're both those things," Jared agreed. "That does not mean I want you in prison."

Mel recognized quickly that he needed to get the conversation back on track. "Gloria, what were you and Carl arguing about?"

"What we always argued about," Gloria replied, playing with the huge sapphire ring on her finger. "He didn't think I was paying enough attention to him. He was extremely needy, if you must know. He made a big deal about not being the center of attention the night before when we were at a charity event. I told him he was being ridiculous and then he accused me of flirting with his son."

Jared made a face. "Excuse me?"

"You heard me." Gloria's expression was dark. "Carl wasn't the easiest man to get along with. I'm sure you've already figured that out, though, unless you're complete and total morons ... which I haven't ruled out. He thought he was in competition with everyone and that included his son."

"We met Junior yesterday," Mel noted. "He said he spent very little time with his father and didn't even seem all that sad at his passing. He didn't mention spending time with you and said he barely knew you."

"Oh, well, I can't speak to that aspect of their relationship," Gloria said primly. "I wasn't privy to the inner workings of their father-son dynamic. I know that Junior wasn't exactly fond of his father because of something that happened with his mother."

"Yes, he screwed his mother out of every penny in the divorce and left her destitute," Jared drawled.

"How did he manage that?" Gloria was officially intrigued. "I wish I would've known that he could do that. I would've hired him as my attorney instead of dating him if I knew that were the case."

Phil slid her a sidelong look. "Do you have to be such a pain?"

"Apparently I do." Gloria made a sniffing sound as she smoothed the front of her cream-colored shirt. "It doesn't matter, though. I dated him. It was casual. I really had no reason to kill him. I mean ... I didn't care about him enough to kill him. If I was going to kill anyone it would be Phil."

"Oh, you say the sweetest things," Phil deadpanned.

Harper glared at her parents. "Knock it off."

"Gloria, you're in real trouble here," Mel noted. "You were the last person seen with the deceased. On top of that, we have a witness who says you arrived an hour before Jared and Harper made it to the house. Even when you take into account the bad roads that day, that means you were inside a full thirty minutes before you called for help."

Gloria was taken aback. "Who told you that?"

"It doesn't matter." Mel was firm. "What matters is that you were there a long time before you called Harper. Why is that?"

"Because ... because ... ." Gloria turned a pleading set of eyes to her daughter. "Are you going to help me here?"

"Help you what?" Harper asked blandly. "I don't know how to help you. It's a legitimate question. Why were you at the house so long before calling us?"

"Even if it took you a few minutes to walk through the house and find the body, we're talking twenty-five minutes here, Gloria," Mel prodded. "What were you doing in that time?"

"I was in shock," Gloria answered. "I mean ... you saw him. I couldn't wrap my head around what I was seeing. I didn't know what to make of it. I thought I was trapped in a dream."

"Obviously you weren't," Mel argued. "What were you arguing about?"

"I told you. He thought I was flirting with Junior at the party the night before. I told him that was ridiculous – the boy is younger than Harper, for crying out loud – but he wouldn't believe me. He said he was going to confront Junior and then he called me a woman of loose moral fiber.

"I threw a pillow at him when he said that," she continued. "A pillow. That's not enough to hurt him. After that, I left. I didn't come back until the next day. I certainly didn't kill him over that."

"What about Junior?" Jared asked. "Did Carl say anything about confronting him?"

"Yes. He said he was going to call him, although I have no idea if he managed to get him on the phone."

"Well, great." Mel rolled his neck until it cracked. "This just keeps getting wonkier and wonkier."

"You can say that again," Jared muttered, his heart skipping a beat when Harper finally met his gaze. She looked beaten down. "I don't think we're even close to being done digging."

"That right there is a fact," Mel agreed. "The question is: Where do we go next?"

Eleven

J ared tracked down Harper in the lobby after the interview
ended. She stood at the front window, her expression
thoughtful as she stared out.

"Hey." Jared was gentle as he rested a hand on her arm.

Harper arched an eyebrow as she glared. "Hey?"

Jared pulled back his fingers and frowned. "I know you're angry," he
started. "This isn't what I wanted. I would throw myself on a grenade
to keep you from feeling what you're feeling now. You know that."

Harper's expression was neutral as she regarded him. Finally, she
folded her arms over her chest and started tapping her foot. "What is
it you think I'm angry about?"

The question caught him off guard. "What do you mean? You're
angry because your mother is a suspect."

"No. I'm angry because you didn't tell me my mother was a
suspect."

"I ... you ... what's the difference?" Jared was genuinely flummoxed.

"The difference is that you should've told me that you thought my
mother was a murderer."

Jared balked, his frustration on full display. "I don't think your
mother is a murderer. That's not what this is about. I didn't have a

choice but to take her in, though. You know that as well as I do. For crying out loud, she was seen — and heard, for that matter — having a fight with Gibbons hours before his death. We can't simply ignore that no matter how much I love you."

"I don't expect you to ignore it. I also don't expect you to pretend everything is fine and lull me into a false sense of security. You should've told me how things would go down."

"You know I couldn't do that." Jared's temper flared despite his unhappiness. "I can't run procedural necessities through you simply because we're going to be married. That's not how this works."

"I didn't say you had to run things through me."

"No, but you're acting like it." Jared went on the offensive because he didn't know what else to do. "You're the most important thing in the world to me. You know that. You are not, however, in charge of how I do my job."

"I don't want to be in charge of your job."

"What do you want?"

"Nothing you can give me right now." Harper was purposely cold as she took a step away from him. "Am I to believe that you will not be arresting my mother for murder tonight?"

"No. She's not under arrest. We will probably have to question her again."

"Well, then ... I guess that means you have more interviews to conduct this afternoon, huh?"

"We do. We're heading back to Junior next. It seems he might've left a little information out when we questioned him earlier."

"I hope you find what you're looking for."

Jared was not a fan of her remote tone. "Where are you going?"

"Are you asking for my official or unofficial itinerary?"

Jared wanted to shake her. "Please don't punish me for doing my job."

She stared at him for a long beat, her expression unreadable. Finally, she just shook her head. "I have things I have to do. I'll be home later."

"What things?"

"Things to help my mother."

"You're not going to get yourself in trouble, are you?"

Harper glared at him. "Don't worry about what I'm going to do. Worry about what you're going to do. There's a real killer out there. No matter what you think, my mother is not capable of doing what you suggest."

"I don't believe she is either."

"Well ... then I guess it's lucky for me that we're on the same side."

"We are." Jared was insistent. "I'm always going to be on your side."

He was so earnest he melted some of Harper's resolve. She didn't outwardly relent, though. "I guess I'll see you later."

"You will," he agreed. "I want you to be home tonight. We need to talk."

"We definitely need to talk," she agreed. "You don't have to worry. I'll be there."

That was the one thing Jared opted to hold on to.

"HOW IS HARPER?"

Mel waited until he and Jared were in his cruiser and on their way to Fran's house to speak with Junior to ask the obvious question.

"She's mad," Jared replied, his gaze focused out the window.

"I'm sorry to hear that."

"That makes two of us."

"You don't have to give me so much attitude," Mel lamented. "It's not my fault this happened."

Jared was incredulous as he glared at his partner. "Why are you playing the victim in this? I don't understand."

Mel balked. "I'm not playing the victim."

"You most certainly are. You're acting as if I'm being unreasonable when it's my life that's threatening to explode. It's my fiancée who is crushed and struggling to stay upright. It's my family that is in danger of falling apart. This is not about you."

Instead of reacting with anger, Mel barked out a laugh. "Oh, you're so full of yourself." He was amused as he shook his head. "Your family is not in danger of falling apart. You're not going to lose Harper, no matter what you keep telling yourself. Stop being dramatic. Everything is going to be fine."

"How can you possibly know that?"

"Because I've seen you and Harper together. No two people were ever destined more for each other than the two of you. She's just upset ... and you can't blame her for that. Her mother is a suspect in a murder and her parents are acting like morons and having sex in your house. That's a lot for one person to deal with."

"I almost think she'd be willing to watch her mother get locked up if it meant she would never have to think about the sex again."

"See. Things aren't so bad." Mel grinned as he regarded his partner. "You can't fix this for her. You both have to go through it together. Give her a little time. She'll get over herself and then everything will be roses and kisses between the two of you again."

"Do you really think so?" Jared was hopeful, but he didn't want his partner to see the fear also lurking in his eyes.

"I do. She just needs time to decompress. In a few hours, she'll be okay."

"She left with Zander. I'm worried he's going to get her riled up."

"Oh, he's definitely going to get her riled up." Mel was matter-of-fact. "After that, she's going to deflate like a leaky balloon. Zander knows exactly how to handle her. There's a reason they've been together since kindergarten."

"I guess." Jared rubbed his cheek. "I don't like it when she's mad at me."

Mel chuckled. "Oh, son, you'll learn to relish fights like this. Once you've been married as long as me the quiet is something to welcome ... and the making up is worth a few hours of unhappiness. Trust me. You guys are going to be fine."

Jared fervently hoped that was true.

"WHERE ARE WE GOING?"

Zander made a face when Harper parked on a nondescript residential street, killed the engine of her car, and immediately exited the warm vehicle and started moving toward a house.

"Hey!" He was offended when she didn't immediately answer and smacked his hands on top of the car to get her attention before she could disappear. She'd been a real pill since they left the police station twenty minutes before — morose, pouty, and furious — and he was at his limit with her silence. "Where are we going?"

Harper paused and regarded her best friend as he pinned her with a plaintive look. "This is Carl Gibbons's house," she said finally.

"Oh." Zander pursed his lips. "Obviously you're looking for his ghost."

"He's the only one who can officially clear my mother right now."

"Not in the eyes of the law ... and Uncle Mel. Only you can see him. I mean ... ." Zander trailed off, understanding blooming. "Oh, geez. You're starting to wonder if your mother is truly capable of killing someone, aren't you?"

Harper was horrified by the question. "Of course not."

Zander waited for her to continue.

"I don't think my mother is a murderer," she said, trying again. "That's not who she is. She doesn't like dirt and grime. There's no way she's going to stab someone."

Zander felt unbelievably sad for his best friend. "You're upset because you think she's capable of murdering someone. I agree about the dirt thing. She's unlikely to want to cause a mess. She's the type of person who could compartmentalize a murder and not even feel guilty about it, though. I happen to agree with you on that front."

"She's my mother." Harper was plaintive. "I'm not supposed to wonder if she's capable of killing another human being. In my heart, I'm supposed to somehow know that she would never do anything of the sort."

Zander blew out a long-suffering sigh. "That's fairy tale talk, Harp. We live in the real world ... at least most of the time. Your mother is capable of killing someone. We're capable of killing people, too, if it comes to it.

"No, we're not capable of murdering someone for no good reason, but we would kill to protect one another," he continued. "I have no doubt about that ... and neither do you."

"That's different."

"Maybe. It's not all that different when you really think about it, though. Your mother could kill under the right circumstances. They're simply not the same circumstances we could kill under. That's not necessarily a bad thing."

"It feels like a bad thing to me."

"Yes, well, you're going through a crisis." Zander peeled himself away from the car and joined his best friend in the middle of the road. He was rueful as he slung an arm over her shoulders. "We're going to get through this." He was calm. "You need to vent, and I get that, but this isn't Jared's fault." He took himself by surprise when he said the words. It wasn't often that he felt the need to take up for the police detective who changed his world ... and potentially in a detrimental way. "He feels really bad."

Harper narrowed her eyes, suspicious. "Since when are you on Jared's side? I thought you hated him because he stole me from you."

"No one can ever steal you from me." Zander was firm. "I'm the king of all men and you can't bear for me not to be in your life."

"That's true." Harper rubbed her nose. "Seriously, though, why are you taking his side?"

"Because he's upset ... and he loves you ... and he's doing the best that he can." Zander opted for sincerity. "He's the love of your life. He's hurting. You're hurting. You need to come to a place where you can hurt together ... and move on together."

"I thought you were leaning toward the idea of me moving out of the new house and in with you and Shawn," she challenged. "This could be the best way for you to get what you want."

"No, it couldn't." He shook his head. "You love Jared beyond reason. He loves you, too. This ... this is just a temporary setback. We'll clear your mother and then everything will be back the way it should be."

"And what if it's not?"

"I don't let ridiculous 'what if' scenarios take up residence in my brain."

"That's probably why people insist you live in La-La Land."

"If you think I'm going to take that as an insult, you're wrong. I'm fine with living in La-La Land."

Harper heaved out a dramatic sigh. "I just ... hate this."

"He hates it, too. He's terrified he's doing you real harm, though. I saw it on his face when he was in the interrogation room with you. He's afraid, Harper, and that's not fair to him. You need to suck it up and make nice with him."

"Fine. I don't want him suffering. I don't want to suffer either, though. He wasn't completely perfect in this entire thing."

"He wasn't," Zander agreed. "You need to meet in the middle."

"Fine. We'll meet in the middle. Are you happy?"

Zander chuckled as he kissed her forehead. She honestly was one of his two favorite people in the world and that would never change. "Yes. Let's see if we can find a ghost, shall we? It would be helpful if we had another suspect to focus on."

"Now you're talking."

FRAN OFFERED UP A WIDE SMILE when she saw Jared and Mel on her front stoop. Her lips curved down after a few seconds, though, when she realized how unhappy they looked.

"Should I be afraid?" she asked after a beat.

"I don't know." Mel decided to be straight with her because the woman had been through so much already. "We need to talk to Junior again. Is he here?"

"He's in the living room." Fran wiped off her hands on a towel and ushered the two men into the house. "Are you going to arrest him?"

"I don't believe that's on the table at this time," Mel replied. "We do have a few questions for him, though."

"This way." Fran's expression was hard to read as she led the two detectives through the house. "Junior is a good boy. Whatever has upset you ... well ... I'm certain he can explain it."

"I truly hope so, ma'am." Mel meant it. The last thing he wanted to do was hurt Fran again after everything she'd been through.

Junior sat on the couch in the living room, a large folder open in front of him. He arched an eyebrow when he realized who was visiting. "Did something happen?"

"A few somethings," Mel said as he sat in the chair across from the couch. "We brought Gloria Harlow in for questioning."

"I see." Junior's emotions weren't on display as he waited for Mel to continue. He was shuttered and in control.

"The neighbor says she heard fighting the day before your father's body was found," Mel explained. "It was Gloria and your father. Gloria threw a pillow at him."

"I doubt that killed him," Junior pointed out. "I've never heard of a thrown pillow being listed as a cause of death."

"That didn't kill him," Mel agreed. "It does make us wonder if the fight continued until later in the night, though. Gloria says she left."

"And you don't believe her?"

"Actually, we believe she left," Mel replied. "The neighbor said she stormed off. The question is: Did she come back?"

"Do you have evidence that suggests she came back?"

Jared made a face. "You're acting more like Gloria's lawyer than the deceased man's son. How come?"

"I'm merely trying to figure out what happened to my father, the same as you," Junior replied simply. "I have trouble believing Gloria killed him. She clearly wasn't in the relationship for the long haul."

"We brought her in for questioning all the same," Mel noted. "We had no choice."

"And what did she say?"

"That she and Carl were arguing about you."

Whatever he was expecting, that wasn't it. Junior finally showed an emotion ... and it was surprise. "Me? Why would they be arguing about me?"

"Well, according to Gloria, she spent some time talking to you at a charity event the night before and Carl wasn't happy about it," Mel responded. "Apparently Carl thought you were flirting with her."

Junior snorted. "You can't be serious."

"And yet ... ."

"Well, I don't know what to tell you," Junior said after a beat. "I'm an intern at the circuit courthouse. I was at the charity event because it was frowned upon to skip the event. I did talk to Gloria, but it was only because I felt it rude to ignore her. We only talked for a few minutes."

"And your father didn't act as if his nose was out of joint regarding the interaction?" Jared queried.

"He didn't. He seemed fine. I'm not sure why he would think I would want to flirt with Gloria. I mean ... she's old enough to be my mother."

Jared had to bite the inside of his cheek to keep from reacting. He could just picture Gloria's expression if she heard the derisive way Junior phrased the comment. She would melt down. It would be more abhorrent than being accused of murder. He almost wanted to tell her as a form of payback given how things were currently going in his life. He knew that would only make things worse, though.

"The way Gloria made it sound, your father was the competitive sort," Mel prodded. "Is it possible he simply wanted to believe you were interested in Gloria because that would mean he bested a younger man?"

"I guess." Junior looked legitimately confused. "I don't know what to tell you. Gloria wasn't flirting with me. I would tell you if she was. She didn't even seem all that interested in having a conversation with me. I think she did it because it was expected. I certainly wasn't flirting with her. I mean ... she's okay, but she's not exactly my type."

"I can see that." Mel rubbed his forehead. "I can't remember if you told us before and I don't have my notes handy. How many times did you meet Gloria?"

"Technically I've met her three or four times, but I only spent time with her once while she was dating my father."

"How have you met her more times?"

"She's a regular fixture in lawyer circles. She seems to date a new divorce lawyer every month."

"Ah." Mel made a face as he turned to Jared. "What do you think?"

"I think that Carl sounds a little nutty," he answered, thoughtful. "Either Gloria is lying about his reaction or Carl was incorrectly over-reacting to things that weren't really happening."

"Which do you think is true?"

"I don't know. We need to find out, though."

"Definitely, although I don't even know where to start."

Twelve

C arl was moping around his backyard when Harper and Zander tracked him down. Even though he was an equal partner in GHI, Zander tended to let Harper handle the heavy lifting when it came to ghosts. He focused on the books and being her wingman when a dangerous job came up. Since he couldn't see ghosts like his best friend could, that seemed like the wisest course of action. That didn't mean he was going to allow her to hang around in a dead man's yard with a killer on the loose.

"You're back," Carl noted when he saw Harper. He almost looked relieved. "I've come to a conclusion, by the way. I'm dead."

Harper worked overtime to maintain a sense of calm as she regarded him. "I believe I told you that yesterday."

"I know, but I wasn't ready to hear it."

"And now?"

"And now I'm interested in hearing your answer regarding ghost sex. If I can't look forward to that, I might as well curl up in a ball under that bush and never move again."

Harper arched an eyebrow and glanced at the dormant lilac bush he gestured toward. "Well, that's certainly an option," she said after a beat.

"What's an option?" Zander asked, stomping his feet on the snow-packed earth to garner some warmth. "Can't we force him to join us in the car? I mean ... seriously. This is inhuman."

"Carl is upset because of the lack of sex in his future," Harper volunteered.

"Well, I can't really blame him there. I would be upset, too."

"He wants to know if ghost sex is a thing," Harper added.

"That's kind of gross. I mean ... well ... is it a thing?" Zander changed his opinion on a dime. "I would kind of like to hear the answer to that."

"See!" Carl puffed out his ethereal chest. "It's not just me. People want to know stuff like this."

"Oh, whatever." Harper pressed the heel of her hand to her forehead to center herself. "I need to know if you've given some thought to your death, Carl. It's important that we figure out who killed you."

"I have given it some thought." Carl was grave. "I know exactly who killed me."

"You do?" Hope welled in Harper's chest. "Who?"

"It was a conglomerate of people I beat in the court system." He lowered his voice to a conspiratorial whisper. "They want me to pay because they were on the losing end of my magical presence and that's how I ended up here."

Harper blinked several times in rapid succession. "Did you make that up in your head?" she asked finally.

"No. It's a real thing."

"It is not."

"It is, too."

"It is not."

"It is, too."

"It is not!" Harper practically exploded. "A conglomerate of the people you beat in court didn't join together to kill you. It was a specific person."

Carl made a sniffing sound. "There's no need to be rude. I believe I've been through enough without having to put up with your attitude. I'm the one who is dead."

"I'm sorry." Harper held up her hands in defeat. "I don't mean to hurt your feelings. It's just ... your neighbor says that my mother was here the night before you died. She says that you and my mother were arguing. Do you remember that?"

Carl's expression turned thoughtful as he considered the question. "I don't know. Who is your mother again?"

If he wasn't already dead, Harper would've throttled him on the spot. "Gloria Harlow," she gritted out.

"Oh, right." Carl brightened considerably. "You're much more attractive than your mother. Has anyone ever told you that?"

"What did he say?" Zander asked when Harper's expression turned murderous. "Did he say anything good? Please tell me he cleared your mother."

Harper ignored the questions. "Carl, this is important. Do you remember arguing with my mother?"

"Vaguely," he replied after a moment's contemplation. "I seem to remember having a brief kerfuffle. I don't believe it was a big deal, though. A pillow might've been thrown. She certainly didn't kill me."

Harper was ridiculously relieved to hear him say it even though she already believed the exact same thing. "Great. That's good."

"Although ... she was only going home for a little bit and then she was coming back. I can't quite seem to remember her coming back. I guess it's possible she killed me during her return visit. She was the only one I was expecting, after all."

Harper frowned. "What? Are you saying she was supposed to come back?"

"Yes. She had a few errands to run. I was going to pop a Viagra while she was gone so I could wow her."

Harper slapped her hand over her eyes, which was a ridiculous gesture because her ears were what were currently being offended. "Oh, my ... I don't need to hear about your Viagra habits!"

Zander snorted. "Oh, did he need the little blue pill to romance your mother? That is so ... wait. Ask him how he expects to have ghost sex if he needs Viagra. I very much doubt anyone is manufacturing ghost erection pills."

Harper glared at him. "Is that important right now?"

"They don't make ghost Viagra?" Carl was beside himself. "That has to be a mistake. Who can I talk to if I want to rectify this situation? It can't be allowed to continue."

Harper suddenly felt weary as she glanced between the whiny ghost and her shivering best friend. For the first time in a long time, she felt helpless. The last time she could remember feeling that way she was walking through a field, looking for the ghost of her dead boyfriend. Sure, that boyfriend turned out to be alive and a criminal, but at the time she didn't know that.

Back then, she used to feel helpless quite often. She had no idea what she was going to do with her life or how she was going to move forward. Luckily for her, that was no longer the case.

"You need to think about what happened to you, Carl," Harper admonished. "It's important. You were killed and there's a murderer on the loose. He or she could strike again. Do you want that?"

Carl held his hands palms out and shrugged. "I can't decide why I'm supposed to care. I mean ... I'm already dead. If others die it's no longer my concern."

"You're all heart, Carl. Has anyone ever told you that?"

"No, and I would smack them if they did. A heart gets you nothing but trouble. I'm a survivor."

Harper found his response laughable. "You're not a survivor. You're dead."

"Well ... you know what I mean."

And, because she did, all Harper could do was nod. "Think about the night you died," she ordered. "Think about what happened after my mother left. Something happened. You were killed. I would think you're not the sort of man who will just sit back and allow that to happen without consequences. I mean ... don't you want payback?"

Carl didn't immediately answer. Instead, he stared at her so soulfully Harper was convinced he was going to finally say something of merit. When he did open his mouth, she was more disappointed than ever. "You're hotter than your mother. I wish I would've met you before I died. We could've had some real fun."

She glowered at him. "Think about who killed you! I'm serious. I don't want to hear another bit of nonsense about your non-existent libido. If you needed Viagra, it doesn't count."

"You tell him, Harper." Zander hunched down in his coat. "Now, can we go? I can't take another second of this cold."

"Yeah, yeah, yeah. We're going. I'll be back, Carl. You better have done some thinking by the time I swing around again. I'll be mad if you don't."

"Is that supposed to scare me?" Carl drawled. "Mad women are something of a hobby of mine."

"You've never met a woman like me before. Think about it. I'm serious. I need to know who killed you."

"I'll think about it ... as long as you ask the powers that be about ghost Viagra. I think it's only fair."

"Consider it done."

JARED WAS EXHAUSTED WHEN HE returned home after his shift. On a whim, he stopped by the local diner long enough to pick up two chicken pot pies — they were favorites for both Harper and him — and he was filled with trepidation when he rounded the corner that led to the house. The relief he felt when he saw Harper's car in the driveway was profound. That feeling only lasted until he realized he had a fight in front of him, though. Then he deflated.

It was time for round two.

Jared paused by the front door long enough to kick off his shoes and remove his coat. The living room was empty, which caused his heart to ping, but some of the stress he'd been carrying for the better part of the afternoon evaporated when he found her in the kitchen.

"Hey, Heart."

She turned quickly. She hadn't heard him enter the house. She was surprised by his stealthy feet. Even more, she was upset by the look of fear on his face. "Hi."

"How was your afternoon?" He rested the pot pies on the counter.

"It was a waste of time. Zander and I tracked down Carl again. He's a dirty pervert. There's no other way to describe him. He keeps talking about ghost Viagra and I really do want to kill him all over again."

For some reason, her insistence on talking about a ghost encounter as if it was a normal day made Jared feel better. "Everyone we've talked to said he was a terrible guy. There is no one we've found who holds him up as a paragon of virtue."

"That's because he's gross."

"Yeah, well ... ."

Harper tilted her head in the direction of the pot pies. "What's that?"

"Our favorite pot pies." He was rueful. "I thought comfort food was a necessity."

She chuckled, catching him off guard. "I thought the same. I got bread bowls from the diner, clam chowder, and cheesecake."

"What kind of cheesecake?"

"Pumpkin."

He laughed. "I guess we both went with the comfort food, huh? Now I kind of want clam chowder."

"I want all of it." Harper rubbed her hands over the front of her pants to dry her sweaty palms. "Before that, though ... I'm sorry."

Jared cocked his head, unsure he heard her correctly. "What?"

"I'm sorry," she repeated. "How I treated you this afternoon, it wasn't right. I'm really sorry and I hope you can forgive me."

He didn't know what to say. "I believe that's supposed to be my line."

"Why are you sorry?" she asked, guileless. "You're not the one who flew off the handle for no good reason. You're not the one who acted like a big baby."

Her words were more comforting than anything else she could've offered him at that moment. "Baby? You're not a baby. She's your mother. You have a right to be upset."

"Not at you." Harper's eyes were clear. "You were doing your job. I can't expect you not to do your job. It's not fair."

"Life isn't fair. I should've told you that it was likely we would have to take your mother in for official questioning."

"Why? It's not my business. You're a police officer. That means you have to explain yourself to the public, not to me. Besides, I've been around enough police investigations that I know the drill. It's definitely not fair that I attacked you the way I did ... and I'm sorry."

Jared forgot about the pot pies ... and the clam chowder ... and the misery he'd been carrying around for the better part of the day. He moved around the counter, pulled her to him, and inhaled her scent as he wrapped his arms around her. "I love you."

"I love you, too." Everything inside that had seemed so rigid only seconds before unclenched as Harper let loose a long sigh. "I'm sorry."

"Don't." He pressed a kiss to her forehead. "You don't need to be sorry. I'm sorry."

"You definitely don't need to be sorry."

"Fine. Nobody is sorry."

They clung to each other for several minutes. Finally, when they pulled apart, Harper was rueful. "We're okay, right?"

"We are." He smoothed her hair. "I have some things to talk to you about. We had another conversation with Junior and I thought you would want to hear his take on things. For the record, he doesn't believe your mother is a murderer."

As if finally remembering Gloria had been living under their roof, Jared gripped Harper's shoulders and stared toward the hallway that led to the guest bedroom. "Are they here?"

She chuckled at the abject horror winding over his features. "No. Dad took her to his house because I exploded all over them when I came back and found them in our kitchen. Mom was going to make liver and onions."

Jared's expression soured even further. "Because she hates us?"

"She claims otherwise, that it's healthy, but I have my doubts." Harper pressed her head to Jared's chest and basked in his warmth for a long beat. "Dad promised to keep her out of trouble for a bit. I have no idea if he's capable of that, but I need a break from them."

"You and me both." Jared tightened his grip on the thing that mattered most to him. "I know I'm supposed to keep opinions like this to myself, but it's a miracle you're normal. Your parents are so screwed up I can't believe you're not locked up in a home."

"Yeah, well ... I would like to lock them up in a home."

"Perhaps we can make that happen after we get past the current maelstrom."

"I'm all for that." Harper shifted so she could brush a kiss against the corner of his mouth. "This is nice. I'm glad we made up."

"Me, too."

"I'm really hungry, though. I haven't eaten since breakfast."

"That makes two of us." He planted a loud kiss on her lips and then released her. "Let's eat pot pies and clam chowder in bread bowls, stuff ourselves with cheesecake, and tune out the rest of the world. How does that sound?"

"Good ... as soon as you tell me what Carl's son said."

"Ah." He tapped his temple. "I should've known you would want to hear more about that. How about I tell you while we're getting everything ready and then we put it behind us, at least for tonight?"

"I think I can live with that."

"Good." Jared moved to the counter so he could start unboxing the pot pies. "Carl Jr. says that he's met your mother a few times. Only once when she was with his father, though, and they never had what could be constituted as a meaningful conversation."

"I'm not sure I understand." Harper donned padded oven mitts so she could retrieve the bread bowls she was keeping warm in the oven. "How did he meet her?"

"Apparently your mother makes the rounds in lawyer circles."

"Ah." Harper made a face. "Yeah, I should've seen that coming. I have no idea why my mother is so insistent on dating lawyers. It's ... weird."

Jared chuckled. "I know why she does it. They're snakes in the grass. She doesn't want to become attached to any of them."

"That doesn't make sense. She's always looking for a soulmate."

"I'm pretty sure she's already found him."

"Who?"

Jared stared at her a beat, dumbfounded. "Your father," he said when it became obvious that Harper couldn't see what was right in front of her face. "Your mother is still in love with your father."

Harper was flabbergasted. "That is the most ridiculous thing I've ever heard. She is not."

"Oh, she is." Jared refused to back down. He was determined to get everything out in the open and put it behind them. "Harper, I know it's freaking you out, but the fact that your parents are still doing it on a regular basis despite being separated explains a heckuva lot. They're still in love with each other.

"That's why they're fighting over the cuckoo clock and a very old Department 56 plate collection," he continued. "They don't really want those things. They simply want to remain entwined in each other's lives. The second they run out of things to argue about, they'll admit it to each other and get back together."

"That is ... ." Harper wanted to argue with him. She wanted to say that he'd lost his mind. The more she thought about it, though, the more confused she felt. "Do you think it's possible that they have real feelings for each other?"

"Of course."

"But ... they've always hated one another. Even when I was little, they hated one another."

"Have you ever heard the saying that it's a very fine line between love and hate? Your parents are proof of that. They love and hate one another."

"But ... I don't understand how this even happened." Harper was at a loss. "If they love each other, why not be kind to one another? It works for us. It could work for other people, too. That probably sounds schmaltzy to say, but I believe it."

He chuckled as he carried the pot pies to the table. "Your parents aren't us. They thrive on the drama. We like a little drama in our lives, too. That's what we have Zander for. They don't have Zander so they create their own drama. I don't think they're ever going to outgrow it."

"Do you honestly think they should stay together?"

"It doesn't matter what I think. It matters what they're going to do ... and they aren't going to allow you or me to lodge an opinion on their lives. All we can do is sit back and watch the train wreck."

"I guess." Harper didn't look convinced. "I'm glad we don't need their brand of drama. I prefer hammocks and pot pies."

He grinned. "You and me both. We can't force your parents to do what we want, though. The faster you come to terms with that, the easier it will be to push your annoyance with them to the back burner. You can't dictate who they are."

"I guess." She rubbed her forehead. "Let's stop talking about them for a bit. Let's start talking about us instead. How does that sound?"

"Like music to my ears. Let's stuff ourselves with comfort food until we're going to burst and then go to bed."

Harper cocked a dubious eyebrow. "You want to go to bed at seven?"

"Yup. We need to finish making up in the bedroom."

"Ah." Her smile was sly. "I guess that can be arranged."

"I thought you might say that."

Thirteen

Harper woke in a cocoon of warmth. She was draped around Jared, his arms tight, and they were buried in covers.

His mouth was ticklish on her neck as he woke her with zest.

"I take it you're feeling frisky," she noted as she found her voice. "I didn't think that was possible after last night."

"We've never really fought before," he noted as he rubbed his cheek against hers. "I thought we should go overboard making up. That's the right thing to do."

"It is, huh?"

"Definitely." He kissed her jaw. "I don't want to get up. I wish we could stay in bed the entire day, shut out the world and eat cheesecake while wearing nothing but smiles. I don't suppose that's possible, though, is it?"

"No."

"I didn't think so." They lapsed into comfortable silence, snow flitting past the window. It would only leave a light dusting behind. It was beautiful from their vantage point, but they would have to join the real world eventually, and then it would be a nuisance. "I have an idea for you today."

"Oh, yeah?" She laughed. "I think I'm kind of tired from the ideas you had last night."

"Not that. I love your dirty mind, though." He gave her a soft kiss, reluctant to let the morning slip away from them. "I want you involved in this and you can't do certain things because of your mother. However, Junior is going to be coming into the office today and going through some of his father's files. We've asked him to recall any stories his father might've told him about the clients — apparently Carl was a braggart of the utmost order — and I thought you might want to go through the files with him. You might recognize some of the names."

Harper was instantly suspicious. "You want me to go through files with Carl, Jr.?"

"I want you to go through files and see if you can pick up on any red flags."

"That doesn't sound like something you would normally want."

"Well ... I'm eager for you to be involved in this process."

"Okay. Why else?"

He blew out a long-suffering sigh. "You're so much work." He tickled her ribs and caused her to giggle — a sound that warmed him to his very core — and laughed as she squirmed. "Does there have to be another reason?"

"I sense there's another reason."

"Yeah?" He met her gaze. "That's why I love you. You're beautiful and brilliant. There is another reason."

Harper was practically salivating. It had to be good for him to be drawing things out the way he was. "What's the reason?"

"I want to know what you think of Junior. I also want you to see if you can get him to trust you enough to confide in you."

That wasn't what she was expecting. "I don't understand," she said after a beat. "Don't you trust him?"

"I do. It's just ... he's Carl's son. You said yourself that the man was a shark. His ghost is still a jerk. There's every chance Junior inherited something other than a pair of dark eyes from his father."

"Oh." Realization dawned on Harper and she propped herself on an elbow as she ran several possibilities through her head. "Do you think he's covering for his mother? Do you think she finally snapped fifteen years after the fact and decided to take out the jerk who screwed her over so badly? If so, I've got to tell you, I can't say I want her locked up. He kind of had it coming."

"I agree." Jared moved his hands to the back of her neck and started rubbing, causing her to moan.

"That feels so good."

"Keep making those noises and we'll genuinely never get out of this bed."

"That's not much of a threat."

"Yeah, well ... as for Fran, I don't know that I believe she's capable of killing Carl. She seems far too nice and sweet. I've seen nice and sweet women lose it, though. If she did snap, I think it's far more likely she hired someone to kill him than did it herself."

"How? She doesn't have any money."

"Yeah, which is why I want you to spend some time talking to Carl Jr. He might know of some money she's got hidden away or something."

"And you think he's just going to volunteer that information to me?"

"Probably not. He's a very controlled individual, though. He never says anything without thinking about it first."

"I think that probably makes him smart," Harper noted. "I never think about what I say before it comes flying out of my mouth and I've lived to regret it a time or two."

"As have I. I simply don't think it's possible to be controlled every second of every day. He might let his guard down with you because you're so cute."

Harper made a wry face. "Why else?"

"Your mother was dating his father. He might be curious about you. If that's the case, he's more likely to share information."

"Ah. You want me to complain about my mother and see how he reacts."

"Pretty much."

"Such a dastardly plan." She smacked a kiss against his mouth. "I'll do it, but you're going to owe me payment later tonight."

"Oh, yeah?" He arched an eyebrow. "What did you have in mind?"

"Well ... I was thinking chocolate cake and pot roast. You know how I love the pot roast at the diner."

"I thought maybe you were going to request something dirty."

"Maybe I plan to request that right now."

"Ah, well, I think we're about to come to a meeting of the minds."

"Somehow I knew you would say that."

TO HARPER'S SURPRISE — and chagrin — Carl was in the police station lobby when she followed Jared through the front door two hours later. She was so taken aback, she let out a squeak ... and then she glared.

"What are you doing here?"

Jared glanced around, confused. "Who are you talking to?"

She scanned the lobby to make sure they were truly alone before answering. "Carl is here. I was surprised to see him."

"Ah." Jared furrowed his brow. "What is he doing here?"

That was a good question, and Harper was curious herself. "He hasn't answered that question yet." She looked to the ghost expectantly. "Do you want to tell me what you're doing here?"

Carl was haughty. "Not that I think it's any of your business — you're kind of a bossy thing, you know — but I followed my files here."

"You followed your files here?" Harper wrinkled her forehead as she repeated the words. "Oh, your files. You mean the files from your office, right?"

"I do." Carl puffed out his chest. "I can't say that I'm happy about Stanley just turning over my files without considering what's right for my clients."

"He's probably betting that one of those clients — or, more likely, the spouse of a client — killed you. If that's true, won't that be better for the client in question because the ex will be going to prison for the rest of his or her life?"

"That is a very good point. Still ... we're not supposed to willingly turn over files this way."

"I think they got a warrant." Harper looked to Jared for confirmation. "You got a warrant, right?"

"We did."

"See. You have nothing to complain about." She pinned Carl with a serious look. "Absolutely nothing."

Jared smirked as he put his hand to the small of her back and prodded her into the conference room. There, four huge boxes of files sat on the table ... and somehow made the space look tiny because they took up so much room.

"Holy moly." Harper was taken aback. "You don't expect me to go through all those files, do you?"

Jared cast her a sidelong look and shrugged. "I thought you wanted to help."

"Oh, puh-leez." She let loose a derisive look. "You're not fooling anybody. You just want me to do the boring work."

"I'm pretty sure I should be offended by that remark."

"And I'm pretty sure this is an obscene number of files." Harper strolled to the edge of the table and pulled the top off the first box. "I mean ... there's like fifty files in here and each one is jam-packed with notes. It's going to take me forever to go through all these."

Jared couldn't help agreeing with her. That didn't mean he was going to let her off the hook. "Think of it as a bonding exercise. We're working together."

"No, you're going to be out interviewing people and I'm going to be stuck here with Carl, Jr. How is that a bonding exercise for you and me?"

"Because I'm going to massage you until my fingers fall off later tonight as thanks."

"That's a start." Harper pulled out the first file and flipped it open, her eyes going wide as she read a transcript. "Son of a ... this is the file for Laura Dorchester and her ex-husband. Do you have any idea how many times she claimed he cheated on her?"

"I have no idea who she is," Jared said blankly.

"He cheated on her seventy-three times," Carl announced, his grin turning evil and reminding Harper of the Grinch. "Because of that — and we managed to prove without a shadow of a doubt he was a serial philanderer — Laura got sixty-five percent in the divorce. That's practically unheard of."

"She got sixty-five percent?"

Since Harper was focusing on what appeared to be thin air to Jared, he assumed Carl was still with them. "You know, having Carl here might be helpful. He can tell you what clients threatened him."

"He can," Harper agreed. "When his son gets here, however, I won't be able to ask him questions."

"That's not happening for another hour. You can get a jump on things."

"Whoopee." Harper gave the boxes a dubious look and then heaved out a sigh as she removed her coat. "You are going to owe me big time."

"I know. I'm going to help here at the start. I'm hoping we come up with a list of people for us to interview."

"Well, if this first file is any indication, you're going to have more suspects than you can shake a stick at. Although ... I've never really gotten the meaning of that saying."

"I know what it means." Carl's hand shot in the air. "Would you like me to demonstrate?"

Harper was confused ... until Carl started gyrating his hips. "No. I have no intention of seeing your ... stick. Why do you have to be so gross? It's no wonder you were killed. The only thing that's surprising is that it didn't happen sooner."

"You've got that right." Jared glared at the empty space. "Don't hit on my girl. She doesn't like it."

"Look at this macho man," Carl teased, rolling his eyes. "He thinks he's actually talking to me. I mean ... come on."

"He *is* actually talking to you," Harper pointed out. "He knows you're there even though he can't see you."

"Yeah, but ... ." Carl trailed off. "I don't like where this conversation is going. We should talk about something else."

"You mean I'm right and you don't want to admit it," she corrected. "I know how you are. It doesn't matter. Let's focus on the files and go from there, shall we?"

"Fine. I'm eager to find my killer."

"Since when?" Harper challenged.

"Since I'm curious to find out how I died ... and get some of that ghost Viagra you promised me."

Harper wisely kept her mouth shut and instead plucked out a file to peruse. She had a feeling it was going to be a long day.

"THIS IS MICHAEL PITMAN," she said an hour later, rubbing her forehead to stave off an oncoming headache. "We went to high school together. Apparently he's fathered two children that no one knows about ... including Corbin Barton, who I thought was the son of another classmate."

Jared glanced over her shoulder — they'd moved to the floor so they could spread out the files and create stacks — and furrowed his brow as he read the top page of the listing. "Michael was Carl's client and he didn't want the woman he was divorcing, one Nan Pitman, to know he'd been running around on her. It looks like Carl helped pay off the mothers of the two children Michael fathered on the side to keep their mouths shut until after the divorce."

Harper turned a set of murderous eyes on Carl, who had mostly lost interest in the conversation regarding his legal prowess. "You're disgusting. You know that, right?"

"What?" Carl wasn't in the mood to make apologies for his behavior. He was long over that. "He has a right to procreate with as many people as he wants."

"Oh, really?" Something occurred to Harper as she studied the annoyed ghost. "Did you have children outside of your marriage with Fran?"

Jared jerked up his head, intrigued. "Good question, Heart."

"Ugh. Did he just call you 'Heart'?" Carl made an exaggerated face. "Could you guys be any more vomit-inducing?"

"We could try," Harper warned. "It's a serious question. Did you have other children? I mean ... one of those kids could've been angry at you and arranged for you to take a header into the living room floor."

"Oh, I get what you're saying." Carl's eyes gleamed with intrigue. "Alas, I was very careful about procreating. I've known where babies come from since I was a kid. After Junior, I knew I didn't want to add to the bills I already had to pay. I had a vasectomy ... and then didn't tell Fran."

"You are a king amongst ... dogs," Harper muttered, shaking her head when Jared shot her a questioning look. "He had a vasectomy."

"Oh, well ... ." Jared chewed on his bottom lip as he studied the fact sheet in Harper's hand. "Do you think your old high school buddy is capable of killing Carl?"

Harper immediately started shaking her head. "He was a big wuss. He married Cindy Monaghan, though, and she was definitely capable of killing him."

"I can vouch for that," Carl added, turning his eyes to the conference room door when it opened to allow Junior entrance. "Look who it is. It's about time he showed up to help."

Harper kept her eyes on the living man and forced a smile as Jared introduced them.

"I thought she could help," Jared explained, gesturing toward the boxes of files. "We're going to have way more suspects when we finish than I thought."

"I'm fine with her helping." Junior's smile was shy as he lowered himself to the ground and studied the piles Harper was creating "What's the organizational process here?"

"This small pile is people who probably don't want to kill your father. This much bigger pile is people who would gladly have snapped his neck."

"Ah." Junior's lips quirked. "I know it's not funny but ... my father was a character. He would probably be thrilled to know that everyone is making such a big deal about him."

"That shows what you know," Carl barked. "I was a big deal so I didn't need anyone to do anything that wasn't genuine."

Junior didn't as much as look in his direction so Harper forced herself to keep from looking at the morose ghost. "I'm sorry I'm late," he offered as he grabbed a folder from the pile Harper was currently working her way through. "I had to stop by my father's house so I could get a copy of his will from the office and his filing system was such a mess I couldn't find it. I guess I'm going to have to go through his probate attorney."

"That's okay." Jared's gaze was on the file he held. "We've already been in touch with his probate attorney. It's some guy named Elliot Taubman. We need to put in a request through the judge — which requires the medical examiner filling out paperwork — and then we can get a copy of the will. Apparently it was updated two weeks ago, which means there are additional hoops to jump through."

Junior stilled. "Updated? What did he update?"

Jared shrugged. "I have no idea. You're his only child, which makes me believe you'll get the bulk of his estate. Maybe he had some charitable organizations in there or something."

That didn't sound likely to Harper, who flicked her eyes to Carl and found him watching his son with gleeful eyes. The older man was so excited, she couldn't hold back the wave of dread that washed over her. "Did your father tell you he was leaving everything to you?" she asked after a beat.

"We never talked about things like that," Junior replied. "I don't even know what his finances looked like. It's possible I won't get anything because there's nothing to inherit."

He said the words, but Harper had a hard time believing them. "Your father strikes me as the sort of person who would leave his money to someone else just to be a jerk," she noted, causing Jared to slide his eyes to her. "Have you considered the possibility that he did have money and he decided to keep it from you because he was ... horrible?"

Junior blinked several times in rapid succession and then shrugged. "I guess it doesn't matter over the long haul. I've made it this far in life without his help. It's probable I will have to make it the rest of the way without him doing the right thing, too."

"Yeah." Harper briefly rubbed the back of her neck and then turned back to the files. "It would almost be easier at this point to make a list of the wronged individuals who didn't want to kill him. This is going to get unruly before it's all said and done."

"I don't doubt that," Jared said. "We have to keep pushing through, though. I don't see where there's anything else we can do."

Fourteen

Harper liked Junior.

Well, to be more precise, she was impressed with the fact that he seemed to be a normal human being despite what a terrible father figure he had in his life. Jared was right about him being thoughtful and easy to converse with. He was also guarded, and no matter how Harper tried to draw him out of his shell, the man refused to talk about anything that didn't have to do with the task they were wading through.

"I'm going to run to the vending machine," Harper offered about two hours into their records search. Jared had left not long after Junior arrived so he could start placing calls. "Would you like anything?"

"Oh, well, you don't have to do that. I can get my own beverage."

Harper kept her expression neutral even as she wanted to blurt out the obvious question. *Who uses the word beverage?* It was odd to her. "I'm going to get something for myself. I would be happy to get something for you, too. It's no big deal."

"Oh, well, if you don't mind." Junior's smile was sheepish. "A Coke would be great."

"No problem."

Harper's mind was busy as she let herself out of the conference room. She found Junior's demeanor stiff but there was nothing unfriendly about the man. In fact, there was every chance his mother had raised him to be polite to a fault, the exact opposite of his father.

"He's boring as sin, huh?" Carl leaned against the vending machine as Harper fed dollar bills into it. "He has way too much of his mother in him. I was hoping he would turn out more like me. He's the reason I only have the one kid."

If Carl boasted a body, Harper wondered if she would be able to stop herself from kicking him in the testicles. "He's easy to get along with," she countered. "Stop being a jerk. He's ten times the man you are."

"You barely know him."

"I know enough. He's way more pleasant to be around than you."

"He's boring. Don't kid yourself." Carl made a face as he inclined his chin in the direction of the hallway behind Harper. "Here comes your boyfriend."

Harper glanced over her shoulder and smiled as Jared closed the distance between them. "Hi."

"Hello." He swooped in and gave her a kiss, not caring in the least that he was supposed to be working and Mel could be watching. "How are you?"

"My butt hurts from sitting on the ground and I'm already tired of reading files. Other than that, I'm just peachy."

"I'm sorry." Jared immediately reached for her shoulders and gave them a squeeze. "You don't have to keep going if you don't want to. I just thought ... ." He left it hanging.

"You thought you wanted me close because we had a bad day yesterday," she finished, understanding perfectly well. "It's okay. I want to be close to you, too. I'm not complaining. Er, well, I'm not complaining a lot."

He chuckled as he pulled her in for a hug. "You don't have to keep going through the files. It's not your job."

"It's not Junior's job either."

"Junior has no life," Carl pointed out as he watched Jared with dark eyes. "He's kind of neutered, huh? He basically does whatever you want because he only cares about making you happy. What a loser."

Harper shot the ghost a death glare. "Shut up!"

Jared arched an eyebrow. "Excuse me?"

"Not you." She patted his chest and went back to selecting drinks from the vending machine. "I cannot stand our friendly neighborhood ghost. He's a complete and total tool."

"Ah." Jared made a face as he stared at the empty spot where she glared. "I don't know how to fix this for you. It's not as if I can beat him up."

"You can't do anything." Harper selected a Coke for Junior and a Diet Coke for herself. "He's just a jerk. You should've seen the look on his face when Junior mentioned the will. I think he did something bad with that will, by the way. I would recommend talking to his estate lawyer as soon as possible."

"Really?" Jared was officially intrigued. "Ask him what he did with the will."

"I can hear you myself," Carl challenged. "I don't need her to tell me what to do."

The look Harper shot him was withering. "What's the deal with your will?"

"Don't worry about it."

"I don't understand why you're being evasive. They're going to find out eventually."

"Well ... good for them. Until then, it's none of their business."

Harper made a disgusted sound deep in her throat and shook her head. "He won't say. He's acting like it's a big deal, though."

"Then I guess I need to track down that estate lawyer after all. I assumed he left everything to Junior. It's not as if he was dating your mother long enough to leave her anything ... and he has no other children."

"He had a vasectomy and didn't tell Fran because he's the world's biggest ... I can't even think of a word bad enough to describe him."

"I'm sure you will come up with something by the time I get back." He pressed a kiss to her forehead. "Until then ... I'm off to see an estate lawyer."

"Good luck."

Harper offered a half-wave as Jared left to collect Mel.

"They're going to see Elliot." Carl barked out a raucous laugh. "They're going to have so much fun."

Harper didn't like the sound of that.

ELLIOT TAUBMAN WORE AN EXPENSIVE suit and what looked to be the world's cheapest toupee. It was so distracting that Jared found he had trouble tearing his eyes away from it.

"Did you say something?" Jared asked when he realized the room was completely silent and Elliot and Mel were watching him.

"I asked if you were the one engaged to the ghost hunter," Elliot replied, amused.

"That would be me." Jared shifted in his chair and forced himself to look away from the bad hairpiece. "Harper."

"I'm mildly familiar with her," Elliot said. "Mel and I used to golf together in a league and he often had Zander and Harper with him when they were kids. They were odd little ducks."

Jared wasn't sure how to take the comment. "She's a beautiful soul."

"I'm sure she is. When she was a kid, she and Zander were terrors. They used to run Mel ragged ... although that was more Zander than Harper and he didn't seem to mind."

"Oh, I minded," Mel intoned, making a face. "There simply wasn't much I could do about it. My mother doted on them ... as did my sister. It was either kowtow to their whims or live in fear."

"Hey." Jared extended a warning finger. "There's no way my Harper was ever the terror you're describing."

Mel's smile was rueful. "You're right. Zander was definitely the terror."

"He's still a terror."

"And I doubt the two of you are here to talk about Zander," Elliot noted. "Is this official business?"

"It is," Mel confirmed. "It's about Carl Gibbons."

"I figured as much. His death has been all over the news."

"It must be a slow news cycle."

"That and the fact that Carl was a notorious figure in certain circles," Elliot acknowledged. "He made a lot of enemies over the years

... and he was proud of it. I've known him for twenty years and he loved bragging about the people he'd screwed over for the duration of that time."

"No one we've talked to has been especially fond of him," Jared agreed.

"I would like to say that he was misunderstood and very few people knew the real Carl, but with him, what you saw was what you got. He was a bad man and he didn't care that people knew that about him. There is nothing that can explain away the horrible things he did."

"We understand that you're handling his estate," Mel noted, digging in the pocket of his coat. "We have a warrant and want to see Carl's will."

"I have no problem with that." Elliot didn't even bother checking the warrant to make sure everything was in order. "The thing is, I don't have his most current will. I only have the one he filed with me two years ago."

Jared was understandably confused. "What do you mean? Why wouldn't you have the most recent will? Did he go through someone else?"

"No. I gave him the paperwork. It's basically a template. He said he wanted to fill it out himself and that he would get it back to me when he was finished."

"How do you know he finished?"

"He called and said he had. He even had it signed by a notary. He was going to send me a copy, although I don't know if he ever got it in the mail."

Jared rubbed the back of his neck, a myriad of possibilities going through his head. "Do you know what he was changing about the will?"

"He didn't say. He was adamant about it, though. He said the old one wouldn't suffice and he needed to do it right away."

"And when was this?" Mel queried.

"He told me he wanted to change the will two months ago. I sent him the template. About a month ago he said he was finished and had to get it notarized. About two weeks ago he sent an email and said he'd finished everything up and would be sending out the new paperwork any day."

"And you never got it."

"No."

"Well ... that's something of a coincidence, huh?" Mel looked to his partner. "What do you think?"

"I guess we can't know what the new will said unless we find it and I don't remember seeing anything close to that when we searched the office."

"No. I guess that means we need to know about the first will," Mel said. "What can you tell us about that?"

"It was fairly standard ... when you take into account the fact that Carl had more than a million dollars hidden in secret bank accounts."

Jared's mouth dropped open. "A million dollars? I don't understand. Did he make that serving as a divorce lawyer?"

"If so, I definitely went into the wrong field," Mel groused.

"Carl wasn't a normal divorce attorney," Elliot explained. "He was a coveted attorney because he was willing to play loose and fast with the rules. He demanded twenty percent of every divorce decree he won. A normal divorce attorney takes ten percent. Carl, on the other hand, got bigger settlements for his clients and they were willing to pay him more."

"I guess so." Mel let loose a low whistle. "A million bucks is probably a motive to kill someone."

"Perhaps, but I'm not sure most people realized that Carl had that much money," Elliot noted. "He liked to play as if he was a big shot, but he also came across as a braggart. He knew that. He played into it. He wanted some people to think he was making up how much money he was worth because it benefitted him."

"I can't believe he was worth a million bucks and he managed to get out of his marriage without giving his wife a dime," Jared muttered, disgust washing over him.

"That's not entirely true," Elliot cautioned. "He gave Fran fifty grand and the house. Granted, he hid all his assets and the house was underwater at the time so there was no way she could keep it, but he didn't get off exactly scot-free in that divorce."

"That's not the way Fran made it sound," Mel argued.

"She put all the money she got into Junior's education," Elliot explained. "She didn't benefit in the least from being married to Carl. Junior, however, got an education out of it."

"That's something Carl should've been willing to pay for no matter what," Jared pointed out.

"I happen to agree with you." Elliot held up his hands in capitulation. "Like I said, I'm not pretending that he was a good guy. In fact, he was pretty much the worst guy I've ever known. All he did was talk about money and sex. Apparently he was a dynamo in the sack."

"Thanks to Viagra," Jared countered, taking perverse satisfaction in outing Carl's secret after the fact.

"That wouldn't surprise me in the least." Elliot looked amused. "Fran wasn't the only one who Carl screwed, though. The guy was notoriously cheap. He also screwed over his own mother."

"Seriously?" Jared knew he shouldn't be surprised, but he couldn't stop himself. "How did he do that?"

"Well, she had a stroke about five years ago, and instead of putting her in a nice assisted living center while she recovered, he put her in a county home ... which was essentially the Devil's armpit, although not as nice."

Jared felt sick to his stomach. "Oh, geez. Is she still there?"

"No. She got out when she recovered. She's not completely living on her own, though. She has an apartment in that building over by the county seat in Mount Clemens. It's assisted living but minimal oversight."

Mel furrowed his brow as he tried to picture the building in question. "That one that looks like it's sagging on one side?"

"That would be the one."

"Ugh. And she's there?"

"She is. If you want insight into Carl, I would start with her. She was in Carl's will before he changed it. I have no idea if she still is."

"What about Junior?" Jared asked. "Was he in the will?"

"He was," Elliot confirmed. "He was getting the lion's share of the inheritance, meaning he should've gotten about seven hundred thousand dollars. Carl's mother was supposed to get another hundred grand."

"That doesn't seem like much considering what he put her through," Mel noted.

"I honestly don't think Carl cared about things like that," Elliot explained. "When he first sat down and we were going through his options, I suggested it might be a nice gesture to leave something for Fran. I never knew her well. She always seemed nice, though. She was kind of timid and I felt bad for her. Carl was having none of it, though. He said she didn't deserve anything."

"The guy had no loyalty," Jared complained, remembering the way Harper warned him about Carl's smug attitude. "Do you think it's possible he took Junior out of his will?"

"When dealing with Carl, anything is possible. The thing is ... I don't know what he would do if that's the case. Carl was not the type of guy who wanted to donate to charities and he didn't have a significant other that I'm aware of. The only two people he had to leave money to were his mother and Junior."

"Speaking of that, were you aware of his relationship with Gloria Harlow?" Mel queried.

Jared managed to rein in his temper and keep a bland expression on his face ... but just barely. He wanted to shake his partner even though he knew Mel was merely asking the questions that needed to be asked.

"I'm aware of his relationship with Gloria," Elliot confirmed. "I thought it was a weird pairing. Everyone in the county knows Gloria. She is ... all kinds of wacky." He remembered that Jared was going to be Gloria's son-in-law at the same moment the younger detective shifted uncomfortably in his chair. "Oh ... I'm sorry."

"It's fine." Jared heaved out a sigh. "I've met Gloria. I know she's not exactly the easiest woman in the world to deal with."

"That's putting it mildly," Elliot said. "She's got a certain reputation in lawyer circles. She likes to date them but not commit. In fact, anyone of a certain age who is looking for a good time is advised to go to her because everyone knows she's not in it for the long haul."

"That is lovely," Jared deadpanned.

"I'm just telling you how people look at her." Elliot was sympathetic. "I'm not saying Harper is like her. In fact, everyone I know happens to adore Harper. She's the exact opposite of her mother."

Jared wasn't sure if the statement was meant as a compliment, but he decided to take it that way. "Harper is an angel."

"Let's not go overboard," Mel countered. "As for Gloria, did Carl say anything about his relationship with her?"

"They hadn't been dating all that long."

"No, but they'd been together at least a month. You mentioned you talked to Carl two weeks ago. Did he say anything?"

Elliot swallowed hard and darted a look in Jared's direction. He was clearly uncomfortable. "Just that he was having a good time, that Gloria liked fine dining and never argued about going to bed with him."

Jared pressed his lips together and raised his eyes to the ceiling as he tamped down his frustration.

"Anything else?" Mel asked.

"Just that. I very much doubt he was going to add Gloria into his will. There would be no reason. He knew the relationship with Gloria wasn't going to last over the long haul. He was simply enjoying the time they had together and then had every intention of moving on."

"That also seems to be the general consensus regarding Gloria's relationship intentions," Mel noted. "If that will shows up, I would appreciate knowing what's in it. As it is, we're going to have to go over his computer and do another search. A will change is definitely a motive."

"I wish I had more information to give you," Elliot offered. "The thing is, Carl talked big, but he shared very little about himself. I have no idea who would hate him enough to kill him."

"That's what we have to find out. Thank you so much for your time."

Fifteen

Agatha Gibbons was a formidable woman, which was quite impressive because she didn't clear the five-foot mark and if she weighed a hundred pounds, Jared would've been surprised. That didn't mean she was the sort of woman who could be taken advantage of ... and she recognized Mel and Jared for what they were the second they appeared at her door.

"I guess I should've realized you would get to me eventually," she said, shoving open the door and gesturing for the detectives to enter her small assisted living apartment. "Come on. We might as well get this over with."

Jared and Mel exchanged quick looks but did as she asked.

Agatha pointed them toward the living room and sat in a well-worn chair — one that looked to be her favorite — and inclined her chin at the couch. "Sit. I know you're here about Carl. I figured you would get to me eventually."

"We weren't even aware you were alive, ma'am," Mel admitted. "You weren't listed on Carl's 'in case of emergency' information. You don't live in Whisper Cove. I'm sorry for getting our wires crossed."

"I don't care about that." Agatha slid a sidelong look toward Jared before focusing on Mel. "You're clearly in charge," she said. "What can you tell me about my heathen son's passing?"

It took everything Jared had not to dissolve into laughter. The woman was funny. He had to give her that. She was also resigned. She clearly had a strained relationship with her son, but he was still the child of her body ... however badly things had gone between them.

"He was stabbed, ma'am," Mel answered. There was no reason to lie. The truth was out there and she would stumble across it eventually. "Someone went into his home and ended his life."

"I see." Agatha worked her bottom jaw. "Do you know who did this dastardly deed?"

Jared had the distinct impression she was playing with them. That was the reason she picked the words she did. "No, ma'am. We're trying to figure that out. That's why we're here."

"You came to see me because you think I killed him?" Agatha arched a drawn-on eyebrow. "I'll admit that I've considered it a time or two over the years, but I'm not sure I have the strength to pull something like that off."

"You could've hired someone," he pointed out, seeing no reason to placate her. Agatha seemed like a straight shooter and Jared figured approaching her on an even level was the smartest way to go. "You might've hated him enough to hire a professional, figuring you would get something in his will to pay off the shooter."

Agatha snorted. "Oh, please. There's no way my son is leaving me a dime. If I paid someone to kill him that would be money out of my own pocket ... and as you can see, that's money I don't have. Do you really think a professional killer is going to meet me here, agree to kill my son for a future payout, and then just take me at my word that I'm good for it? I very much doubt it."

She had a point. Jared was loath to admit it because he was desperate for another legitimate suspect, but the odds of Agatha taking out her son seemed slim. "I guess that leaves us open to discuss other things." Jared gave her a small wink in the hope that she would relax. Instead, she continued to glare at him ... which made him uncomfortable.

"And what do you want to discuss with an old lady, hot shot?" she challenged, causing Mel's lips to quirk. "Just for the record, you're wasting your charm on me. You're way too young and dumb for me to waste my time on. I don't want a guy I have to teach the ropes to."

Jared was almost certain an insult was buried in there, but he managed to refrain from calling her on her attitude. "I'll keep that in mind, ma'am."

"We're more interested in your relationship with your son," Mel explained. "We just spent some time with his estate lawyer and were informed that things weren't always pleasant between you and Carl."

"That's putting it mildly. Carl was ... pretty much the worst son anyone could ever want. I'm not kidding ...and I'm not exaggerating. He was a jerk and a half."

"That doesn't mean he deserved to be murdered."

"No?" Agatha didn't look so sure. "I'll have to let God be the judge of that. I didn't kill him. If you really think that and aren't just marking off a box on your list, I feel sorry for you. You're wasting your time with me. Even if I wanted to kill him — and there were times, don't get me wrong — I don't have the strength to do it physically. I also don't have the money to do it remotely. That's on top of the fact that I don't have the will to do it.

"Carl was essentially a butt plug in the game of life," she continued, ignoring Jared's reaction when he uncontrollably started coughing to cover his laughter. "I'm not an idiot. I know what my son was. He wasn't a good person and he's going to be on the receiving end of some hard judgment. I have no doubt about that."

"When was the last time you saw your son?" Mel asked.

"I think it's been about two years."

"Two years?" Jared sobered. "He never came to visit you?"

"He hated coming here. Said it was for old people. That's why I pointed out I should be living in a different sort of home. He said I was old and to suck it up, claimed he couldn't afford to put me anyplace else. He said he didn't have a choice ... and I definitely didn't have a choice."

"Your son managed to squirrel away about a million dollars," Mel offered, choosing his words carefully. "A few months ago, he approached his estate lawyer about changing his will. Up until that point, his son was the main beneficiary and you were set to receive one hundred thousand dollars."

Agatha made a face so exaggerated she looked like a cartoon character. "Are you messing with me?"

"No. The thing is, we've yet to track down the new will and have reason to believe he might've done something ... odd ... with it." Mel wasn't sure how else to phrase it. "He didn't mention anything to you, did he?"

"I haven't seen him in almost two years. He didn't even mention the first will to me. I figured everything would go to Junior. That's the way it should be."

"Even though you're living in a home you hate?" Jared queried.

She bobbed her head without hesitation. "Even though. I don't belong here, but Junior has been through so much in his life that if his father can give him a little bit of peace, he definitely deserves it."

"Are you close with your grandson?" Jared asked.

"I don't know if 'close' is the word I would use," Agatha hedged. "Fran stops by to see me once a week. She brings me a casserole. I've never been one for casseroles, but it's the thought that counts, right?"

"Fran visits you every week?" If Jared wasn't already in awe of the soft-spoken woman this would've put her over the top.

"She does."

"For how long?"

"Since I've been in here," Agatha replied. "Actually, when I was in the hospital, she stopped by twice a week to cheer me on during my physical therapy. She also volunteered her time to help me with my speech therapy."

"That's pretty generous of her considering how your son screwed her over," Mel noted.

"I always said that Carl didn't deserve her," Agatha noted. "No, I'm being serious. He didn't deserve her even a little. She was too good for him.

"What Carl did when he divorced her was ... unconscionable," she continued. "I knew that marriage wouldn't last, don't get me wrong. Fran is a sweet woman, but Carl is the sort of man who is attracted to evil.

"Still, I thought Fran was better off without him despite the terrible financial state he left her in," she said. "I thought maybe she would find someone who treated her right ... but that never happened. She seems fine taking care of herself, and Junior is an adult now. She did right raising my grandson. I'll always appreciate her for that."

"And what about Junior?" Jared pressed. "How often do you see him?"

"Not as often as his mother but more often than most grandchildren would probably stop by. He comes about once a month. He brings me a basket of goodies — some are baked goods from his mother but other items are contraband and he buys them for me anyway — and we sit and play cards for an hour or so.

"He tells me about school because he's almost ready to graduate from law school and he's gearing up to take the bar exam," she continued. "He's warned me that he has to study hard for the exam and might miss one visit. I told him not to worry, but he feels bad about it."

"It sounds to me as if Fran made sure that Junior was close to you despite what Carl did to her," Mel said. "She did everything right."

"And Carl did everything wrong," Agatha said. "Listen, my son was a monster. I'm not surprised that he's dead. In fact, the only thing that surprises me is that no one took him out sooner. It wasn't me, though. It's probably one of the people he wronged in a divorce settlement. That's all I can figure."

"We're looking into that," Jared said. "The problem is, he screwed over a lot of people. There are so many names to choose from we don't even know where to start. He never mentioned a name to you, did he? Someone he really messed up maybe. He seemed proud of throwing people's lives into tumult. I thought maybe he would brag about it to you."

"He didn't talk to me unless he absolutely had to," Agatha said. "I'm sorry. I don't know what to tell you. I wish I had more information for you ... but I simply didn't know my son well enough to help."

"That's okay." Jared forced a tight-lipped smile for her benefit. "I'm sure we'll figure it out. Until then, we'll be in touch if we have more questions."

"I wish you well." Agatha's expression was conflicted. "The problem is, whoever killed my son is likely to have a good reason. He or she might have sympathy on their side before it's all said and done. My son wasn't a good person, like I said."

"No, but murder is never allowed no matter how bad the person is. We'll definitely be in touch. You need to take care of yourself, though. That should be your primary goal."

"I'm always worried about myself." She mustered a cheeky grin. "Now, go. Point that charm toward someone else. I'm sure it will be appreciated if you direct it at someone younger."

Jared knew just who he wanted to direct it toward.

"HELLO?"

Jared didn't bother knocking before letting himself into the house Zander shared with his boyfriend Shawn. Until several weeks before, Zander owned the house with Harper. Once the house across the street went on the market, Jared and Harper decided to buy it. That allowed both couples their own space but also made it so Harper and Zander — who were woefully codependent — could spend as much time together as necessary.

Jared was familiar with the house so he didn't feel the need to knock. He was almost bowled over by the heavenly aroma of pot roast when he cut through the house after kicking off his shoes.

"What is that?" he asked, gliding to a stop in the kitchen and lifting his nose. "I think this is what Heaven must smell like."

Harper laughed from a stool at the kitchen island. Zander was behind the counter, an apron covering his clothes, and he was clearly putting on a show for Harper and Shawn as he finished up dinner.

"Don't you knock?" Zander challenged when he met Jared's gaze. "Harper doesn't live here any longer ... thanks to you. That means you have to knock."

"Do you knock when entering our house?"

"That's entirely different."

"How?"

"Because I said so."

"Ah." Jared ignored Zander's attitude and moved to Harper, pressing his cold hands to her neck and making her squirm before planting a solid kiss on the corner of her mouth. "Did you miss me?"

"Every moment of my life spent away from you is terrible," she teased as he gave her another kiss.

"What's up with you guys?" Shawn asked after a beat, his brow furrowed as he watched the adorable exchange. "You guys seem ... off."

"They had a fight," Zander answered for them. "I told you about it."

"Oh, right." Shawn bobbed his head. "Jared took Gloria in for questioning and Harper was upset. I didn't think you guys were still fighting about it."

"We're not still fighting," Jared replied, wrapping his arms around Harper's waist from behind. "We're making up. It's going to be a week-long process. I've already decided."

"A week, huh?" Harper was legitimately amused. "Do you think we'll be able to keep this up for a week?"

"Yup. I think we're going to enjoy it."

Shawn smirked as Zander rolled his eyes.

"What did you find out about the will?" Harper asked, turning serious. "Did you find it?"

"Not yet, but we're still looking." Jared kept his arms around Harper but scowled as he thought back to his afternoon. "We spent hours going through that house and couldn't find the will."

"What about his computer?"

"That is there but it's password protected. The state police are picking it up in the morning and having a tech look at it. Elliot Taubman — he's the estate attorney we talked to — said that Carl had completed his new will. We just need to find it."

"I remember Elliot," Harper noted. "He golfed with Mel."

"He remembers you, too." Jared's lips were busy on Harper's neck. "He says that you and Zander were adorable children but a lot of work."

"He was talking about Zander."

"He was," Jared agreed, chuckling when Zander scorched him with a dark look. "Oh, lighten up. I'm sure you were an adorable kid, too."

"I was the cutest kid ever born," Zander agreed without hesitation. "Parents everywhere wanted to trade their kids for me. My mother had to watch me extra close when we were out because she was afraid someone would steal me."

"It's the truth," Harper added. "He was the child everyone wanted."

Jared had heard so many stories from their childhood he knew that wasn't true. By all accounts, Zander was something of a nightmare to raise. Most people called his mother a saint and then made the sign of the cross to double down when referring to Zander's antics. He knew better than believing his girlfriend's well-rehearsed shtick with her best friend.

"Well, he asked about both of you," Jared supplied. "He seems like a nice enough guy. He admits that Carl was basically the worst. As far as he could tell, Carl didn't have any redeeming qualities."

"I would definitely agree with that," Harper said. "Carl hung around the entire afternoon. He kept throwing passive aggressive digs at his son. Junior, of course, couldn't hear him. I think that's for the best, though."

"How did your time with Junior go?" Jared asked. "Did he let anything slip about his relationship with his father?"

"I'm assuming it sucked given the way Carl treated his mother," Zander said.

"I don't think they had the warmest of relationships," Harper agreed. "He would not, however, go into any detail about his father. I tried like eight different ways. You used the word 'guarded' when you described him and I think that's the best word. He won't say anything bad about his father, which is frustrating because I think that's a subject we could bond over."

Jared snickered. "Yes, well ... what about your mother? Did he say anything about her relationship with his father?"

"Wait." Shawn held up his hand to still the room. "I thought we all agreed that Gloria had nothing to do with this. She's not still a suspect, is she?"

"She can't be ruled out as a suspect," Jared replied, opting for honesty. "Personally, I don't happen to believe she's a legitimate suspect. That's because she would rather die herself than get dirty, though. I don't believe my gut instinct is going to hold up in court if things go south."

"Do you think it will go to court?" Harper looked worried at the prospect.

"I doubt it." Jared stroked his hand down her hair to soothe her. "That possibility is a long way off. We're nowhere close to making an arrest. This will change could be a powerful tool on the motive side. Your mother is lacking in motive."

"What about Phil, though?" Zander asked. He wasn't facing Jared so he missed the dark look that flitted over his friend's face. "If he and Gloria have secretly been together all this time, it makes sense to me that he might be jealous of the men she was dating. Maybe he killed Carl because he thought there was a chance the relationship would last."

When no one immediately responded to the statement, Zander glanced up from his food ministrations and frowned. Harper's glare was hot enough to cause blisters to break out on his skin.

"Or, I could just shut up and cook," he said after a beat.

"I think that would be good," Jared agreed, moving his hands to Harper's neck so he could rub at the tension. "Right now, we're trying to find the will. We know what the old one said, how the funds were divvied up. Now we need to look at the new one."

"Do you think that will be the final clue you need?" Harper asked.

He shrugged. "I don't know. I certainly hope so, though. The sooner we can put this one behind us, the better."

Sixteen

T he snow was coming down when it came time for Harper and Jared to leave.

"Look at that." Harper brushed her fingers against the window and shook her head. "I guess it's good we only have to cross the street, huh?"

Jared moved his hand up and down her back as he considered the scene. "It's still going to be virtually impossible to get your car out. I didn't realize it was snowing this hard."

"Stay here," Shawn suggested, moving behind them. "Harper's old room is still basically her room. We put a new bed in so we can use it as a guest room but there's no reason you guys should have to go out in that."

Jared wasn't happy with the suggestion. "It's only across the road."

"And a little way down," Shawn teased. "You could twist an ankle or fall if you're not careful."

"No. We're heading home. It's literally only three inches of snow, although it looks as if the plow has come by and buried the end of the driveway. We can make it."

"Fine." Shawn held up his hands in surrender. "I just thought Harper and Zander might want to have a slumber party or something."

"I have no doubt that will eventually happen," Jared said. "It can wait until the weather really calls for it." Jared grabbed her hand and dragged her toward the door. "You'll be able to watch us through the window to make sure we finish our trek."

"If we fall, call the police," Harper teased, laughing when Jared tugged her knit cap over her head far enough to cover her eyes. "I'll figure out a way to get my car out tomorrow morning."

"We have a snow blower," Jared said. "I'll handle our driveway and come over to do yours. That should make getting her car out relatively simple."

"That sounds like a plan." Shawn waved as they left, casting his gaze to Zander when he joined him in front of the window. "I tried to get him to let her stay. He was adamant they were going home."

"It's fine." Zander wasn't particularly perturbed as he watched Harper and Jared slip and slide at the end of the driveway. Harper was laughing so hard she bent over at the waist. "They seem happy, right?"

The question caught Shawn off guard. "Yeah. Is there a reason they wouldn't seem happy?"

"They had a fight."

"Couples fight. We fight all the time ... mostly because you're rigid and won't let me decorate."

Zander made a derisive sound in the back of his throat. "That's not even a real fight. That's a fake fight so we can make up. They had a real fight over Gloria."

"I didn't realize it was that serious."

"It's not as if they were in danger of breaking up or anything, but it was a real fight." Zander was thoughtful as he turned away from the window. He had a lot on his mind these days and he was never sure how to prioritize it. "You've met Gloria. You don't think she could be a murderer, do you?"

Whatever question Shawn was expecting, that wasn't it. "Are you really worried about that?"

"I'm ... not sure." Zander moved closer to the window so he wouldn't have to strain as hard to make sure Harper and Jared made it home. He felt weird watching over them as if he were a worried parent, but he couldn't stop himself. "If Jared arrests Gloria and she actually gets charged for murder ... ." He purposely left the rest of the sentence hanging.

"What? Do you think that will be the end of Harper and Jared? If so, I think you're wrong. They can get through anything. Besides, I never got the feeling Harper and Gloria were all that close."

"They're not, but Gloria is still her mother."

Shawn gently rested his hand on Zander's shoulder. "They're going to be fine. I look at them and think anything is possible."

"Yeah?" Zander arched an amused eyebrow. "What do you see when you look at us?"

"Basically the same thing ... although I do wish you would let me help decorate."

"Oh, geez." Zander rolled his eyes. "I told you. It's best if only I decorate. That way everything will mesh together seamlessly."

"And I still believe you're full of crap on that front."

"I'm not, though."

"I think you are."

"Yeah, well ... let's take this in front of the fire and argue over catalogs," Zander suggested. "We can have hot chocolate and really get into things. How does that sound?"

"It sounds like a very pleasant evening." Shawn grinned as he turned back to the scene out the window. Jared and Harper had made it to their house and were busy kissing in the snow before heading inside. "They're going to be fine," he repeated ... and he meant it to the core of his soul. "Gloria isn't a murderer. She's vain, selfish, and out of touch with reality. She's not a murderer, though."

"I know. That doesn't mean she won't be arrested. Harper is going to be in an awful spot if that happens."

"It's not going to happen." Shawn was convinced that was true. "Jared will do whatever is necessary to find out what really happened. He won't just do it for Harper either. He'll do it because he's a good cop. Trust me."

"Yeah." Zander heaved out a long-suffering sigh. "So ... catalogs and hot chocolate?"

"That sounds like Heaven."

. . .

HARPER WAS WARM AND COMFORTABLE when she woke. Jared was snuggled close at her side, his breathing steady. The drapes were pulled back from the window to show off a clear sky ... and at least six inches of fresh snow on the ground. It was the perfect morning ... until she remembered that they wouldn't get to spend the day in bed.

"We need a vacation," Jared murmured as he slid closer to her, his lips brushing the back of her neck. "Where do you want to go?"

Harper wasn't expecting the question. "We could just hole up here for a weekend. Once this is over, let's make a plan to stock up on groceries and shut out the rest of the world."

"I'm always open for that. I was thinking of an actual vacation, though. We've only been out of town twice since we hooked up. Once was to go to Harsens Island, which is literally twenty minutes away so it doesn't count. The other was to an island with a haunted asylum, and that definitely doesn't count. Oh, and we went morel hunting up north that one weekend, but that doesn't count because we found a body."

"Maybe we're just not good on vacations."

"Or maybe we need to try an actual one so we can relax."

Harper pursed her lips as she regarded him. "Like ... where?"

He smiled. "I don't know. I was thinking someplace where we can hammock all day and have fruity drinks with umbrellas on the beach at night."

"So ... tropical?"

"Maybe. I'm open to suggestions."

"It's kind of a nice idea," she admitted. "I don't think I've ever been on a vacation before. Not a real one, I mean."

"Then we definitely need to make it happen."

"Yeah." She trailed her index finger down his cheek. "It can't be until after ... you know."

"I know." He kissed her finger and grinned. "I think as soon as we can arrange something — like the second your mother is in the clear — that we should do it."

"I think that sounds like a fabulous plan."

"Good." He drew her close and spent a moment holding her simply for the pleasure of doing it. Then, on a sigh, he pulled back. "I was thinking that we could dig your car out at Zander's, move it over here, and then you could come with me ... at least for the morning. I'll buy you breakfast at the diner before we start. If you're interested, I mean."

"I'm always interested in breakfast. What do you have in mind for our morning, though?"

He cast her an evil grin, which made her frown.

"Don't be gross," she warned. "We have to be respectable members of the workforce today and you know it."

"You're such a spoilsport." He tickled her ribs. "Do you want to go to work with me for a bit or not?"

"Sure. Although ... what did you have in mind?"

"I have to search Carl's house. I need to find that will. I thought you might be helpful, especially if his ghost is hanging around."

Harper made a face. "I hate him. I don't ever want to see him again."

"I'm pretty sure that's how everybody felt. We have to find that will, though. It might have answers."

"Ugh." Harper let loose a dramatic sigh. "Fine. We'll head over to Carl's house. If he's gross, though, I'm going to zap him over to the other side. I'm not even going to tell you before I do it. I'm just going to whip out a dreamcatcher and that will be it."

"Fair enough."

"You're not going to give me grief about zapping him when we might still need him?" She was instantly suspicious.

"I have faith you'll do the right thing. You always do."

"Oh, that was schmaltzy."

"I do my best."

"You're a master at it."

"I'm fine with that."

CARL'S HOUSE WAS A MESS when Harper and Jared walked through the front door. Papers were strewn up and down the hallway and couch cushions were shredded, the stuffing torn out. Jared immediately held up his hand to halt Harper when he caught sight of the chaos.

"Son of a ... ." He looked around, his eyes wide. "I can't believe this."

"What are we going to do?" Harper's nerves were on full display as she glanced around the house. "Do you think whoever did this is still here?"

"I doubt it." Jared kept her behind him all the same. "Call Mel. Tell him what's going on."

Harper didn't offer up a word of argument, instead digging in her pocket until she came back with her phone. She immediately called Mel, who picked up on the second ring, and explained what happened. Jared remained vigilant until she'd hung up the phone.

"What did he say?"

"He's on his way. He needs to get out of his driveway first, though. It might be a few minutes."

"Okay." Jared was grim as his eyes darted from one side of the foyer to the other. "I think you should go outside, lock yourself in my truck, and wait there until Mel shows up. I'm going to search the house."

Harper was having none of that. "I'm staying with you."

"No, you're not."

"Oh, but I am."

"Harper!"

"Jared!" She mimicked his voice to perfection. "I'm not leaving you so don't even try. We're doing this together."

"Oh, geez. You are so much work."

"Right back at you."

Jared drew his weapon from the holster at his hip and sent her a hard look. "You stay behind me. If I tell you to run ... ."

"Then I'll run," she finished.

He bobbed his head in agreement.

"As long as you're right behind me," she added.

The gaze he shot her was withering but there was nothing he could do. His first priority was to make sure the house was clear. That meant searching every inch. "Just ... be really careful," he growled.

The search was methodical, and completely fruitless. It only took them fifteen minutes to search the structure from top to bottom — there were only so many places a grown human being could hide, after all — and Mel was coming through the front door when they finished.

"What do you have?" he asked, his eyebrows migrating north when he saw the mess in the living room. "What the ... ?"

"The house is empty," Jared replied, his gun holstered again. "We went through every room. Whoever did this is gone."

"Well, it would've been stupid for him or her to stay once the sun rose," Mel noted, glancing around. "I'm guessing that our perp came in during the middle of the night, looked around, and then left. Did you see any footprints walking away from the house?"

Jared shook his head. "I didn't. I wasn't really looking when we walked up, but they would've stood out regardless thanks to the new snow we got."

"Right. Which means that whoever broke in here did it and then left long before you guys arrived."

"Yeah." Jared shifted his eyes between the living room and foyer. "I'm guessing that someone was looking for the new will."

Mel was officially intrigued. "What makes you say that?"

"Well, for starters, that's what we've zeroed in on as a motive for Carl's death — at least right now — and whoever did this was obviously searching for something."

"Maybe he had diamonds hidden here or something," Mel argued. "Someone could've known that."

"Then why not search the house after killing him? There was time. Why not search the house yesterday ... or the day before? Our guy did it after we started asking questions about the will. I don't think that's a coincidence."

"How would this person know, though?" Harper asked. "I mean ... how could anyone know what you were investigating?"

"Actually, I'm betting news got out quickly that we were at Elliot's office yesterday," Jared pointed out. "If it's one thing we've learned since starting this one, it's that lawyers are a gossipy bunch. They talk to each other, about each other, and over each other.

"Elliot was very forthcoming with us when we were talking," he continued. "He said that absolutely no one liked Carl. They made fun of his dating choices, whispered about the way he screwed over Fran, and were basically in awe that he could constantly win the way he did. That means that everyone was gossiping about him on a regular basis, whether for good or bad reasons."

"I guess." Harper moved to a sheet of paper on the floor and bent over to pick it up. "This is paperwork from his house insurance packet."

"I'm guessing that whoever was going through his files simply tossed everything when he or she didn't find what they were looking for."

"I get that but ... isn't Carl's office that way?" She pointed toward the hallway. "I seem to remember that from the search."

"It is," Jared confirmed.

"So ... why is the paperwork here?" She looked to the stairwell. "There are three rooms upstairs, right? Carl turned the master bedroom into his office."

Jared caught up to her train of thought. "Why would the papers end up over here if the search was conducted back there?" He pointed and circled. "If the office was upstairs, then it might make sense for some of the papers to end up down here because they could've fluttered over the railing or something. These papers were tossed from that direction."

"How do you know that?" Mel asked, staring toward the living room, which was the direction Jared indicated.

"Because they fluttered this way." Jared strode into the living room and gave it a good once-over. "Here." He moved to the desk and pulled open the top door. "Yeah. This desk is empty. I always assumed the desk was just for looks, but I'm guessing Carl kept things in here."

"Someone jimmied the lock," Mel noted as he dropped to his knees and studied the antique desk. "There are fresh scratch marks here. I think someone used a tool — probably a butter knife or maybe a small switchblade — to open the desk. The papers were strewn because they weren't important to our perp."

"You need to stop saying 'perp,'" Harper instructed. "It makes you sound like a sad *Miami Vice* reject. I mean, seriously, who says that word?"

"I do and I happen to like it." Mel flicked her between the eyebrows as he planted his hands on his hips. "So, do we think our suspect found the papers he was looking for?"

There was the question, Jared realized. "If so, we might be looking at an even worse problem."

"And what would that be?"

"Well, we're assuming that whoever broke in here did so because they wanted the new will. The theory is that whoever killed Carl didn't want the old will changed. There were basically only two beneficiaries in the old will ... and that makes me nervous."

"Agatha and Junior," Mel intoned. "You think it's one of them."

"You met Agatha. She's not strong enough to kill Carl. She's weak."

"Maybe she really did hire someone," Mel suggested. "She's a feisty old bird. She might've been so open to hating her son in front of us because she figured we would never pin this on her."

"She still would've needed money to hire a hitman," Jared argued. "She acted as if she didn't realize she was included in the first will."

"That's true." Mel was rueful. "I'm not saying that I believe she's guilty or anything. I just don't think we should rule her out until we know more."

"Fair enough. That leaves Junior. Do you think it's him?"

"I really don't want it to be him," Mel admitted. "He grew up to be a strong young man despite having the worst father ever. I would like to believe he's somehow transcended what happened to him."

"He was the one getting the lion's share of the money from that first will," Jared pointed out. "That might be enough to kill for, especially to a guy like Junior who has never even had two nickels to rub together thanks to his greedy father."

"Yeah, well ... I don't know what to think." Mel was at a loss. "We also can't rule out Fran in all of this. If she knew her son was inheriting that money, that might've been enough to tip the scales. She might not have cared enough to kill Carl for her own needs, but I have no doubt she would do what it takes to protect her son. The question is: Would she go this far?"

"I don't want to believe it's her," Jared admitted. "I don't want to believe it's Junior either, though."

"What about Agatha?"

Jared pictured the tiny, brutally honest woman. "I don't know that I can see her doing it either. They're our three best suspects, though. You're right. If it was a client, why break into the house and tear things apart like this? There's no benefit after the fact."

"That's why we have to drill down." Mel was resigned. "I think it's one of the three. We just need to be absolutely sure which one because this is going to ruin a lot of lives."

"I hate this," Jared muttered.

"That makes two of us."

Seventeen

Zander showed up at the house not long after. He didn't bother knocking — or even calling out — before striding through the front door. He made a face when he saw the mess.

"This is what I believe the inside of my brain looks like every month when I have to balance the books," he announced.

Jared shot him a dark look. "You can't just walk into a crime scene, Zander."

"Sure I can. The door was open."

"Yeah, but ... ." He looked to Mel for help but the older detective clearly wasn't interested in being dragged into the conversation.

"Why are you here?" Harper asked. She was sitting cross-legged on the floor going through some of the discarded documents. So far, she'd come up empty. All she'd managed to accomplish was disliking Carl more (if that was even possible) because he came across as a pretentious douche even in his correspondence, which she considered something of a miraculous feat.

"We have a job," Zander replied, wrinkling his nose as he delicately stepped over some of the couch stuffing and moved closer to his friend. "Since we usually don't get jobs this time of year, I thought you would want to jump on it."

"Who?"

"Eleanor Pickens."

Harper stilled, surprised. "You've got to be kidding. The same Eleanor Pickens we gave an estimate to in early December and she decided that she didn't really have a ghost and was perfectly fine putting up with the weird occurrences in her house?"

"That would be the one." Zander's smile was broad. "She's decided she really does have a ghost after all."

"I have no problem helping her," Harper said. "I think we should make her sign a contract before we do it, though. She strikes me as the type to back out when it's all said and done."

"I've already emailed one over. I told her I wanted it signed and notarized before we would do anything about her little problem. She whined about the notarizing but agreed. She'll have the contract waiting for us when we arrive. If she doesn't, we'll turn around. I'm not playing games with that old bat."

"You shouldn't talk about Eleanor that way," Mel chided. "She's a nice woman ... who just happens to be a little nutty at times. I didn't know she had a ghost."

"She claims it's Fred," Harper explained. "It's not, though."

"Her husband Fred?" Mel made a face. "He was pretty lazy in life. I can't imagine him being a real go-getter as a ghost."

Harper snickered. "I never really thought about that, but you're right. She's convinced that he's haunting her because she was a nag. I tried telling her that's not how things work, but she won't listen to me."

"If it's not Fred, who is it?"

"It's her mother-in-law. I caught a glimpse of her when we were there the first time. She's got a little crazy wafting around her, too."

"How did you identify it as the mother-in-law?"

"There was a photo on the wall."

"Ah." The ghost thing was still hard for Mel to wrap his head around. He'd known Harper since she was a small child, believed in her abilities, and was genuinely very fond of her. That didn't mean he could get behind the idea of rampaging ghosts running around and causing trouble. His mind simply refused to accept it. "How will you handle the situation?"

"We'll simply trap her in a dreamcatcher and send her over. I even have one handy." Harper dug in her pocket until she came back with one of the handmade dreamcatchers she designed to help lost spirits cross over. "I thought I might need to use it on Carl, but I guess I didn't get that lucky."

"He's not here, right?" Jared looked around for confirmation. He couldn't see ghosts but there were times he swore he could feel them.

"He's not," Harper agreed. "I don't know where he is. I don't really miss him. I guess I could look later if you want, though. We still need to figure out what's in that new will. He might be the only one who can tell us at this point."

"Don't worry about that ... at least for now." Jared crossed to her and kissed her upturned mouth. "You do what you need to do for work. I don't want you worrying about this. We'll ... figure it out."

Harper wasn't convinced. "What are you going to do?"

"I don't know. We have three suspects. I guess we'll just have to break it down."

"That sounds like a place to start."

WHEN THEY GOT BACK TO the office, Jared and Mel made a plan. They were going to whiteboard everything they had on all their suspects and go from there. That meant Gloria as well, something Mel hated to bring up. Jared barely batted an eyelash when he did, though.

"No, I get it." He was calm as he grabbed a marker and moved to the board. "For all we know, she could've somehow trapped him into changing his will so she's the sole beneficiary. I think she might have that power over certain men."

Mel snorted, genuinely amused. "I would never underestimate her."

Jared blocked off the board into four parts and then started writing. "Okay, under Gloria, we have the fact that she fought with the deceased hours before his death."

"She also returned and was in the house a significant amount of time before calling you," Mel pointed out. "Have we ever figured out why she did that?"

"Um ... no." Jared furrowed his brow. "That's a good question. I haven't seen her to ask. Ever since Phil announced he was taking her to his house until she felt better, I've simply been so happy to have her out from under my roof I didn't think to bother her with questions."

"So, maybe we should call her in here."

Jared shifted from one foot to the other, uncomfortable. "I guess we should do that. She's going to put up a fight."

"Yeah, well, she needs to tell us the truth." Mel was firm. "We could pretty much cut her out as a suspect if it weren't for those two things. I mean ... what are the odds Carl changed his will so she's the beneficiary? He'd only been dating her for a few weeks."

"And the way Elliot made it sound, he was well aware the relationship wouldn't last. He was only in it for the fun of it and had no doubt that it would be over once he got bored."

"That means it doesn't make sense for him to make Gloria the beneficiary."

"No. Plus, Elliot said he contacted him two months ago about changing the will. He only finished the job two weeks ago. He wasn't dating Gloria when he decided to change it."

"Another good point. Hold on." Mel had his cell phone in his hand. "I'm messaging Phil. I told him that we need her in here to answer a few more questions and that she's not under arrest. If he doesn't message back in an hour, we'll go looking for her."

"That should go over well."

"There's nothing else we can do."

Since he agreed, Jared returned to the board. "Next up is Fran." He felt bad for writing down her name, but they could hardly rule her out as a suspect. "She has no alibi other than work. We called and confirmed that she was at work during the run-up to the murder but not during the overnight hours. She left late that evening but had plenty of time to kill Carl."

"You've met that woman. Do you think she's honestly capable of killing Carl?"

"I don't know. I wouldn't think so but ... people have been known to do strange things when pushed to their limits. I don't fancy myself a murderer, but I would kill to protect Harper. What if Fran found out that Carl was going to take Junior out of his will for some reason? That might've pushed her over the edge."

"I can see that." Mel rubbed his forehead as he internally debated the possibility. "I have trouble picturing her doing it in my mind. I mean ... after that first blow, he probably wouldn't have been able to defend himself. If she took him by surprise, I can see that. I just don't know what to think."

"I don't want to believe it's her either," Jared acknowledged. "I don't see where we have much of a choice, though. He screwed her over so badly that she very well could've tamped down her rage for years. Maybe she told herself it would all be worth it because Junior was going to be okay and then she found out the opposite."

"Even if Carl removed him from his will, though, that doesn't mean Junior won't be okay. He's about to finish law school. His grandparents paid for that so he's not in the hole. He seems like a good man who genuinely cares about his mother. Heck, he still visits his cranky grandmother even though I'm going to bet that woman hasn't done a lot for him over the years."

"Yeah, I'm going to bet that, too." Frustration welled up as Jared started making notes. "Technically, we have to list revenge as one of the motives under Fran. I'm willing to bet, if it is her, she did it to protect Junior. She might've figured that was her only shot to make sure he got everything she could never give him."

"Something that will make her a sympathetic figure to any jury," Mel noted. "They might let her off on a manslaughter charge or something."

"While I don't want anyone to get away with murder, I would almost relish it if she did." Jared moved to the next slot on his list. "That brings us to Junior. From his perspective, he might have a lot of rage built up where his father is concerned. I haven't seen anything from him to indicate that, but I think it's entirely possible. Maybe he's adept at hiding it."

"I have to tell you, if my father ever did to my mother what Carl did to Fran, I might have a bit of anger myself," Mel admitted.

"I would've picked a fight with my father a long time ago under the same circumstances."

"We have to take the ransacking of Carl's house into consideration, though," Mel pointed out. "I have to think that means our culprit was looking for something very specific. Was Junior aware of the will potentially being changed?"

"Um ... I can't remember." Jared thought hard. "He was in that room with Harper for hours yesterday. She knew we were going to talk with Elliot. I texted her updates. I guess it's possible she told him."

"But is it likely?"

"No. I can text her, though. It might take her a little bit to get back to me if she and Zander are working but as soon as she sees the message, she'll respond."

"That's good." Mel cracked his fingers and exhaled heavily. "Junior would be strong enough to kill Carl. He probably wouldn't even need to take him by surprise."

"Yeah, but the medical examiner said that there were no defensive wounds on Carl. To me, that seems to indicate that he didn't expect an attack. So, what? Does that mean that Junior walked into his house in the middle of the night, woke him up, and Carl didn't expect anything even at the end?"

"Your tone makes me think you don't believe that's a legitimate possibility."

"I don't. I think if Junior let himself into Carl's house in the middle of the night that Carl would've realized he was in trouble. Of course, there's always the possibility Carl didn't think Junior was a threat simply because he'd beaten him down so much over the course of his life.

"Harper said that Carl was acting smug and superior to Junior, degrading him. She seems to think that Carl got off on being a jerk to his own son," he continued. "If he didn't see Junior as a threat, he might not have been leery if he was the one who showed up that night."

"When did Harper say this about Carl and Junior?" Mel furrowed his brow, confused. "Did she spend time with them I don't know about?"

"No, it happened yesterday."

Mel made a face. "You mean that Carl's ghost was doing and saying things."

"I believe that's what I said."

"And I believe we can't use hearsay from a ghost to make our case."

Jared shot him a quelling look. "Let's not have this argument, okay? I happen to believe Harper. If she says Carl was being dismissive to his son, I see no reason for her to lie."

"I didn't say she was lying."

"No, but you insinuated it. Let's focus on this and I will refrain from bringing up ghosts for the rest of the afternoon. How does that sound?"

"Freaking heavenly."

Jared smirked as he moved to the last square. "That leaves Agatha. She's elderly, recovering from a stroke, and doesn't have the money to hire a hitman as far as we can tell."

"The hitman angle bothers me for a different reason, and it doesn't matter who would've hired him," Mel admitted. "A hitman would've come in and popped him in the head once with a bullet. Maybe he would've used a knife if he wanted to stay quiet and didn't have a silencer. He wouldn't have stabbed him five times, though."

"No, that indicates a crime of passion," Jared agreed. "In my head, I see him arguing with someone. That someone loses his or her head and stabs him. Then they either went into a frenzy or simply wanted to make sure he was really dead so he couldn't live to tell the tale. I'm leaning toward frenzy, though."

"I'm right there with you." Mel's expression was thoughtful as he studied the board. "I think whoever took out Carl that night was enraged. Unfortunately, I don't see how we can rule anyone out given that. With these four suspects, any of them could've lost their minds."

"We have to start whittling them down."

"How do you suggest we do that?"

"I have no idea."

GLORIA AND PHIL STOMPED INTO the police station

shortly after lunch. Gloria's eyes were filled with fire and Phil looked as if he wanted to be anywhere else. Still, he held firm at Gloria's side and didn't back down when she started screeching.

"What is the meaning of the text you sent Phil?" she snapped, her temper on full display. "How dare you demand he bring me here."

"I don't believe that's the way I phrased it," Mel replied calmly. "I simply told him that we needed to speak with you again and asked him to call me so we could set up a time. I had no idea he intended to bring you down here."

"Oh, well, you had no idea." Gloria fanned her face, which was red from exertion. "What do you vultures want now? I mean ... haven't you taken enough from me? I don't have any dignity left. You've stripped it all from me. I'm a bare wreck." She dramatically threw herself into the chair across from Jared's desk.

"Oh, geez." Jared rolled his eyes. "If I didn't know better, I would swear you're Zander's mother. I wondered where he learned that 'woe is me' crap he spouts. Obviously he learned it from you."

"Oh, suck it." Gloria made a face and focused on Mel. "What is it that you want?"

"We have to talk to you," Mel replied. "We need to know what you were doing at Carl's house in the time between when you found his body and when you called Harper."

Gloria was taken aback. "Excuse me? I believe I told you that I was in shock."

"And I don't believe you." Mel was matter-of-fact. "Gloria, you're many things, but you don't shrink in the face of hard times. You did something in that house. I want to know what it is."

She moved her jaw but didn't immediately speak.

"It's important, Gloria," Jared prodded. "It's important to you, of course, because we would really like to clear you. It's most important to Harper, though. It hurts her to think that you could potentially go to jail. Now, I don't care if you enjoy playing games. For once in your life, I would appreciate it if you did what was right for her."

Gloria stared, unblinking, for what felt like a long time. Finally, she heaved out a sigh. "If you must know, I was searching his upstairs rooms for the tickets he bought to the bar association gala next week."

Jared was confused. "What?"

"I don't have time to find another date," she explained. "Besides, I actually paid for those tickets because he was the cheapest man alive. There's no way I was just going to leave them there."

Jared didn't even know what to say so he looked to Mel for help. "Did she just say what I think she said?"

Mel nodded. "Yes. She was looking for party tickets in a dead man's house."

"Oh, well, that's what I thought she said." Jared slapped his hand to his forehead. "Please don't let Harper end up like her twenty-five years from now. Please."

Mel was amused. "Are you praying?"

"Yup."

"If you're going to pray, remind God that I'm forty-four," Gloria said. "I'm only fourteen years older than Harper ... at least as far as everybody else in town knows. I want that rumor to spread and stick for a change."

"Yeah, yeah, yeah. I got it."

Eighteen

Harper was stiff and dirty when she got back to the office to drop off the equipment. She and Zander flipped a coin to see who would be responsible for logging it back in ... and she lost. She wasn't happy, especially since she was the one who did most of the running around at Eleanor's house to catch the ghost, who not surprisingly did not want to be caught.

The ultimate takedown happened in the attic, which was dusty and full of cobwebs. Since he claimed he was allergic to cobwebs – a dastardly lie – Zander refused to do more than stick his head through the opening and shout out encouragement. In the end, it took almost a full hour to trap the feisty mother-in-law, who swore up and down she was only doing bad things to Eleanor once a month as payback for the years she was married to her son.

Harper didn't believe her and a fight ensued. Harper was so relieved when she finally trapped the ghost with the dreamcatcher that she almost took the equipment home without checking it in. She'd only done that once before and somehow lost an expensive EMF monitor in the process, so she knew better.

The office was quiet when she let herself in through the front door.

It was after closing time and Molly and Eric were long gone. She didn't bother locking the front door. She knew she wouldn't be long. Instead, she carried the equipment to the storeroom, marked each item off the list as she returned it to the allocated slot, and then hurried back the way she came.

She was almost to the door before she realized someone was standing on the other side of it ... and it wasn't a ghost.

"Who are you?" It was dark enough Harper couldn't make out his features and she wisely took a step back, internally cursing herself for not taking the time to flick the lock. Zander and Jared would get on her about that ... that is if something terrible wasn't about to happen.

"It's me." The voice was decidedly male, but she'd already figured out that for herself because of his broad shoulders.

"You're going to need to be more specific."

"Carl Gibbons, Jr."

"Oh." Harper let loose the breath she'd been holding and cocked her head to the side. "What are you doing here?"

"I need to talk."

"About?"

He pointed toward the window. "You talk to ghosts, right?"

"Yes."

"I want to talk to my father."

"I see." Harper wisely made sure she kept as much distance between her and Junior as possible as she circled to her desk. She had a taser in the drawer. Jared gave it to her as a gift for Christmas. She had no idea if it was even charged, but she didn't have anything else that even resembled a weapon close enough to grab. "And what do you want to talk to him about?"

"I want to know why he was the way he was." Junior's face was still shrouded in shadows, but his voice was low and mournful. "I want to make sure I don't have it in me to be that way, too. You don't think it's genetic, do you?"

Harper's heart went out to him. At the same time, she didn't trust him. "I don't think that's genetic. If genetics were the most important thing that played into personality I would be chasing lawyers looking for someone to date like my mother or living on the beach so I could get away from responsibility like my father."

"Yeah. You don't have great parents either."

"I don't have terrible parents," she countered, sliding into her desk chair and keeping a firm gaze on a man she desperately wanted to be lost and searching rather than hunting. "You had it much worse in the father department. My father was simply ... goofy. He was there for me most of the time, though. He always had an ear to listen and still does to this day."

"That's how my mother is, although she's not really goofy."

"I don't know your mother. I don't think I've ever met her. Jared has met her, though. He likes her a great deal. He says that most women wouldn't have been able to pick themselves up and start over like your mother did. He said she was remarkable."

"My mother *is* remarkable. She always took care of me, made sure I got the best she could possibly give even if she had to go without herself. I didn't even realize how bad we were off until I was in middle school. She was working eighty hours a week to get by and still trying to help me with my homework when she could."

"Did you ever ask your father why he did what he did?"

"Ask? No. I confronted him when I was in high school. I never told her that, but I did. She was in the hospital. She passed out. Thankfully it was nothing serious. She simply fainted because she was dehydrated and overworked. I heard the doctor telling her she would die if she didn't start taking better care of herself. I was so mad that night I drove to his house and confronted him."

"What did he say?"

"He said that eventually I would learn some people were better than others. He said my mother was one of the people who didn't matter. He said that she would die one day and no one would care. It made me really angry."

"Did you hit him?"

"No. I wanted to but ... I was still afraid of him. By that time I was four inches taller and I'd been working out with the football team. I knew I could've taken him. I was still afraid, though. I grew up afraid of him."

The more Junior talked, the more uncomfortable Harper grew. "Did he ever abuse you?"

"Not physically."

"He did mentally, though, right?"

"Oh, he would never look at it that way." Junior trailed his fingers along the window frame as he looked toward the vast darkness outside. "He told me he was toughening me up. He called me names when I was a kid, said I was a wuss. He called me a 'mama's boy,' as if that was an insult given who my father was.

"I know now, as an adult, that she was the best parent I ever could've asked for," he continued. "I also know that I carry his name. Part of what's inside me came from him. I don't want to be his son."

That's when reality set in for Harper and she abandoned her idea to grab the taser. "Is that why you're here? You want to talk to his ghost and tell him that you'll never be the man he wanted you to be, don't you?"

Junior nodded, and when he turned, Harper realized he had tears glistening in his eyes. "I didn't know you talked to ghosts when I first met you. I mentioned your name to my mother when I got home last night and she knew all about you. She said she saw you on television a few times."

"Yes, I've become quite the celebrity," Harper agreed dryly.

"That's why I came here. I actually wasn't sure I would have the guts to walk through the door and ask for your help. Then I saw you were alone and I figured now was as good a time as any. The thing is, I don't have any money to pay your fee right now. I will, one day, but I would have to give you an IOU until then. If that's not enough, maybe you need some help around the office or something. I don't know what I could do, but I'm sure there's ... something."

A huge ball of guilt smashed into Harper's chest as she immediately started shaking her head. "You don't have to pay me. I'll gladly help you."

"You will?"

"As a matter of fact, your father has been hanging around in his ghostly form. I've spoken to him a few times."

"You have?" Hope flashed across his handsome face. "Is he here now?"

"No. I've talked to him enough to figure out what kind of man he is, though. By the way, he's a crappy man."

"He definitely is," Junior agreed. "What did he say to you?"

"Oh, well, nothing good." Harper wasn't sure how much truth the young man could take. Honestly, though, she didn't think lying would make things better. If she did, she would've done it without a second thought. In this particular case, though, it was best Junior's beliefs be held up rather than torn down.

"He doesn't have anything nice to say about anyone," she started. "The first time I met him he asked if he could have ghost sex with me."

Instead of being embarrassed, Junior's mouth dropped open and he burst out laughing. "Are you serious?" He wiped at the tears in the corners of his eyes. "That's so ... him."

"Yes. That was before he realized who my mother was. When that happened, he asked me with more gusto."

Junior laughed again and this time Harper joined in. "That is the legacy he left me."

"Not entirely," Harper said, sobering. "I don't know if I should tell you this. I'll probably get in big trouble because Jared and Mel will want to tell you, maybe feel you out to gauge your potential guilt. I'm going to tell you anyway."

"My potential guilt?" Junior drew his eyebrows together. "They think I killed my father?"

"No more than the other suspects they have," Harper reassured him quickly. "The truth is, they don't know why your father was killed. It could've been a former client ... or someone related to a former client."

"That's what I was assuming. My father made a lot of enemies throughout the years."

"Yes, but he was stabbed five times. I'm not a police officer, but I've seen enough detective shows to know what that means. You're going to be a lawyer. I think you know what it means, too."

"A crime of passion," he deduced, bobbing his head. "I figured that out myself. To me, though, that doesn't rule out the husband or wife of one his former clients."

"Definitely not," Harper agreed. "However, there is one other thing ... and I just know Jared is going to be mad that I told you."

"Then don't tell me. I'll go to the police station tomorrow and ask him to tell me."

"That would probably be easier. It's just ... well ... I want to tell you."

Junior chuckled. "Then tell me. I'll try to act surprised when Jared brings it up so you don't get in trouble."

"Oh, no. I'll own up to my idiocy. He'll be angry, but he won't stay that way. Besides, he took my mother in for questioning this week. It kind of seems I've got a freebie built in somewhere."

"Fair enough. Tell me the thing."

Harper sucked in a breath. It was now or never. He'd given her an out and she'd blown it off. There was no reason to drag things out. "What do you know about your father's will?"

"We already talked about that," Junior replied, blasé. "I'm not going to be in my father's will. I never assumed I would be."

"But you are. Or, at least you were." Harper explained about the wills, leaving nothing out. When she was finished, Junior looked legitimately surprised. "So, you see, you might have a motive and not even realize it."

"I would never kill for money, not even him."

"I know. I was just saying that because Jared and Mel will argue it when they bring you in for questioning. I want you to be ready."

"There's nothing to be ready for. I didn't know about the old will. I don't really care about the new will."

"You don't want a million dollars? Or, I guess it was originally less than that because he gave your grandmother a hundred grand. Still, though, that's a lot of money."

"It is," Junior agreed. "I plan to make that much money ... someday. Do you know what I'm going to do when that happens?"

"What?"

"I'm going to send my mother on a cruise. She's always wanted to go on a cruise. She claims they're magical."

Harper had never given it much thought, other than from a business perspective. "I heard the rooms on cruise ships are small."

"I've heard that, too. My mother won't care, though. She loves the idea of being on the ocean."

"Well, that sounds like a fabulous gift." She meant it. "You could give it to her now if you inherited that money."

"And trust me, that's something I would do. I would also make it so she could retire ... or at least cut down to forty hours a week."

"That seems fair."

"I don't believe that he was changing that will for my benefit," Junior pressed. "That's not the sort of person he is. You said two months ago? Yeah, I'm pretty sure that's about the time I got in a fight with him about Grandma."

"You fought with him about your grandmother?"

"He was trying to cut her monthly allowance. She gets to stay at the home for free thanks to government assistance, but my father still gives her money each month. It's not much. Two hundred bucks. It's enough for a few treats and she plays nickel poker with her friends at the home."

"And he was going to take that away from her?" Harper was horrified. "Why?"

"He said she didn't need it, that the home gave her everything she needed."

"I take it you argued with him about it."

"I did. I told him that my grandmother gave birth to him, that he wouldn't even be here if it weren't for her, and that he needed to suck it up and be a man."

"And how did he respond?"

"Not well. He called me a few names, one a derogatory term for female genitalia I won't repeat in mixed company, and told me I was too old to be so naïve. He said that I would end up doing the same to my mother. I told him that was never going to happen.

"It didn't matter, though," he continued. "He said he was taking the money from Grandma. He said she was talking smack about him down at the senior center. I guess someone asked if he was really born with both female and male parts. Grandma tells a story where that happened and they let him choose if he wanted to be a man or woman. Then she always adds on that he chose to be a woman."

Harper pressed her lips together to keep from laughing. "I see. That's ... um ... ."

"It's funny," Junior supplied. "You can say it. I know it's funny, too. My grandmother doesn't have much to laugh about, but she absolutely loves that story."

"I can't believe your father would take away her allowance over something like that."

"Yeah, well, he was a jerk."

"Maybe he was taking away more than that," Harper mused, absently scratching the side of her nose. "I don't suppose he would've told her if he planned on cutting her out of his will, would he?"

Junior shrugged. "Why would it matter? I'm sure she assumed he would outlive her."

"Yeah, but he didn't."

Junior's eyebrows hopped. "You're not suggesting my grandmother killed him, are you?"

Harper held out her hands and shrugged. "I don't know. Do you think she's capable of it? I mean ... I know she had a stroke, but if she managed to get one good blow in he would've probably been incapacitated and she would've had an easy enough time finishing him off."

"Yeah, but ... huh."

Harper watched him as the wheels turned. "Can she pick up and leave her home whenever she wants?"

"She can. She does it quite often. She makes runs to the liquor store just because she likes getting the nurses at the home stirred up. They're not supposed to have liquor, although they never take it away from Grandma. I sneak stuff in for her, too."

"So, she could've gotten out of the home," Harper mused. "Do you think your father was mean enough to take your grandmother out of his will just because he was embarrassed?"

"Most definitely. The thing is, I'm betting he took me out, too. He was really mad when I confronted him."

"Well ... how late can your grandmother receive guests?" She glanced at the clock on the wall. It wasn't even seven yet.

"For another hour," Junior replied. "Do you really want to go over there and question her?"

"Yeah, and I want to bring Mel and Jared along for the ride. I think they're going to want to hear this new information."

"Okay, but I'm telling you, there's no way she's capable of this."

"For your sake, I hope you're right."

Nineteen

Jared met Junior and Harper in the parking lot of the assisted living center and the first thing he did when he caught sight of his fiancée was to flick the spot between her eyebrows. She was expecting a hug — and maybe a kiss — so she was understandably taken aback.

"What's that for?" she asked.

"That's for meeting with a guy who could potentially be a murderer after dark without backup."

Harper jutted her lower lip out. "I didn't plan it."

"It's not her fault." Junior raised his hand quickly. "If you're going to be mad at someone, be mad at me. She didn't have any choice in the matter. And, to be honest, I didn't think about it."

"Well, think about it." Jared refused to back down. "She was alone and vulnerable. You could've been a dangerous individual for all she knew. I love her. I don't want her hurt."

"I don't want her hurt either. I have no intention of hurting her, in fact. It's just ... I had some questions to ask and I thought maybe she could help."

Jared rubbed at the mounting tension in his forehead. "Questions about your grandmother?"

"No." Junior was solemn. "Questions about my father."

"And how did you think she was going to answer them? She didn't know your father."

Harper cleared her throat and hopped from one foot to the other. "Um ... the thing is, he's talking about what I do for a living."

Realization dawned on Jared and he felt like an idiot. "Oh." He instinctively moved his hand to Harper's back. "I guess that makes sense. I didn't even think about it." He made a rueful face as he regarded his girlfriend. "Did you help him there?"

Harper shook her head. "Not yet. It's not as if Carl was hanging around my office. I'll have to handle that meeting once things settle a bit. As for now, well, I thought it best we talk to Agatha. The fact that Carl was cutting her allowance is a new wrinkle in the wallpaper."

"He was? Then it is," Jared agreed, drawing his hand through his hair. "I still don't know how she would've managed it. Mel will be here in a few minutes. I want to know everything you know about this situation and then I want the two of you to wait in the parking lot until we're done questioning her."

Harper immediately started putting up a fight. "You can't shut me out now. That's not fair."

Jared cocked an eyebrow. "Life isn't fair."

"Jared."

He wanted to hold strong, cut her out of the final takedown ... if that's what this really was. He wanted her safe and warm at home. One look at her face told him that wasn't going to be an option, though.

"Okay, here's the situation," he said after a beat. "I'm going to allow you to go in with me but you can't talk. You have to let Mel and me handle all the questions. Do you understand?"

Harper nodded gravely. "Yes. I'll be good."

"You'd better be." Jared slid his arm around her shoulders and tugged her close so he could kiss her temple and focused on Junior. "What about you? Do you want in on this? You might be able to help us trap her under the right circumstances."

Junior nodded, thoughtful. "I don't think she did this, but I want to be with you to question her if she did. I ... I guess we'll just have to wait and see."

"I guess we will."

AGATHA WAS IN A HOUSE ROBE and slippers when Mel knocked on the door. The look on her face when she answered was harsh enough to peel the skin of a potato that hadn't been boiled.

"Oh, what do you want now?" she groused, her temper on full display.

"We want to talk to you," Mel replied, his voice light and easy. "There are a few things that have come up."

"I see." Her eyes floated between faces before lingering on Harper. "I know who you are. You're the one who can see and talk to ghosts."

"I am," Harper agreed. "It's nice to meet you."

"I would say the same to you but when you get to be my age, you don't want a ghost whisperer darkening your doorstep."

"Fair enough."

"Why are you here?" Agatha didn't usher them inside, instead glaring from her spot. "I'm getting ready for bed. I don't think I have the time or inclination to be a hostess tonight."

"Grandma, you should let them in," Junior prodded. "They want to talk to you about Dad's death."

"Uh-huh." Agatha worked her jaw. "Fine," she said finally and turned on her heel. "This had better be quick, though."

Harper made sure to lag at the tail end of the group, frowning when she caught sight of Carl. He stood in the kitchen, his expression dour, and barely looked up when the others entered the space. His gaze was fixed solely on his mother.

"She did it, didn't she?" Harper kept her voice low when she asked the question, her eyes boring holes into Carl.

"She's evil," Carl replied, his tone gravelly. "Why do you think I turned out the way I did?"

"I think you made your own decisions and enjoyed being evil," Harper replied without hesitation. "Your son was partially raised by evil and he turned out nothing like you."

"He's weak," Carl muttered. "He's always been weak. Fran made him that way."

"No, he's strong." Harper refused to back down. "He's the man you should've been."

"Yeah, well, I guess we'll find out, won't we?" Carl almost looked sad when he met Harper's steady stare. "I remember what happened."

"Was it her?"

"She surprised me. I thought she was going to disown me, maybe threaten to curse me or something. She used to threaten that when I was a kid. Instead she had a knife. It was already too late when I realized what was happening."

"If only you hadn't tried to screw her out of two hundred bucks a month, huh?"

"She didn't need that money. She was wasting it."

"Who are you to say that?"

"Oh, stuff it." Carl moved away from Harper and positioned himself behind Junior so he could openly glare at his mother.

When Harper turned, she found Mel, Jared, Junior, and Agatha watching her. She straightened quickly, squared her shoulders, and then moved to the chair Jared had left open for her. He clearly wanted to make sure she wasn't in Agatha's swing zone should the woman lose her mind and attack.

"Sorry about that," she said quickly. "I was just ... talking to myself."

Junior's eyes lit with interest. "Were you talking to my father?"

Harper opened her mouth to answer, but Agatha spoke before she could.

"Of course she wasn't talking to your father," the older woman snapped. "Ghosts aren't real."

Jared held Harper's gaze a moment and then cleared his throat. "A few things of interest have turned up since we last spoke. One of those things is that we found out your son cut off your allowance. You didn't mention that before."

"I didn't realize I was under any obligation to mention it," Agatha shot back. "I must have missed the part where you read me my rights."

"We don't need to read you your rights if you're not under arrest."

"Oh, well, you learn something new every day, huh?" She was flippant, but her eyes were keen when they landed on Harper. "Your mother was sleeping with my son. I bet she killed him."

"I don't happen to share that opinion," Harper replied primly.

"Of course not. You're going to side with your mother. I bet you even make up stuff that's supposedly said by ghosts from time to time to make sure people believe the con you're running, huh?"

Harper opted not to answer.

"Ma'am, we're not here to talk about ghosts," Jared supplied. "We're here to talk about Carl and what he did to you. How come you didn't mention that he'd cut you off financially?"

"You didn't ask."

"It seems to me that you had a motive to kill him even though you denied it when we stopped by to see you earlier," Mel interjected, his tone grave. "Not only did your son cut you off financially, but he also was in the midst of changing his will. Were you aware of that?"

"I believe we already talked about that."

"Yes, but now I'm starting to wonder if you were telling the truth." Mel rubbed his palms on his knees and stared at the older woman. For the first time since he'd met her, he saw what she really was. "Were you aware that your son was changing his will?"

"Why would I be aware of that?" Agatha opted for an elusive tone. "I mean ... it's not as if we talked a lot. I told you that. I hadn't seen my son in two years."

"Oh, she's lying," Carl protested, his temper finally getting the better of him as he sputtered. "I told her what I had planned. It was fun. I mean ... it was a heckuva lot of fun. The look on her face when I told her the gravy train had gone dry, well, it was beautiful."

Harper felt sick to her stomach as she shifted on her seat. Jared slid her a sidelong look, a question in his gaze, but she couldn't very well answer with Agatha present.

"Are you positive you didn't see your son for those two years?" Jared queried, playing a hunch. "I mean ... if we check with the front desk, are they going to tell the same story?"

Agatha's expression turned foul. "How should I know? I'm not responsible for them. I only know that I haven't seen him for two years."

"I guess we should probably check on that." Jared slowly got to his feet. "If I go out to that front desk and they tell me Carl has been here in the past two years, you're going to be in a lot of trouble. Is that what you want me to do?"

For a long beat, Agatha met his gaze, unblinking. It was as if she was daring him to take her on. Then, possibly realizing she was out of options, she let loose a long sigh and lowered her challenging glare. "How did you figure it out?"

"We didn't until right now," Mel admitted. "We had a feeling that it was you thanks to something your grandson said. We wanted to be sure, though."

"I'm sorry, Granny," Junior offered, his voice cracking. "I didn't know. I ... thought there was no way it could be you. I still don't know how you managed to do it. I mean ... why?"

"You know why." Agatha didn't look sorry about what she'd done. The only regret present was due to the fact that she'd been caught. Harper had no doubt about that. "Your father was an awful individual. I mean ... just awful."

"That seems to be the general consensus," Jared agreed.

"Oh, that shows what you know," Carl sneered. "I was revered. Other men wanted to be like me and women wanted to get with me."

Harper shot him a derisive look.

"Oh, it's true," Carl intoned. "Your mother couldn't get enough of me."

"Which must be why she had sex with my father five minutes after you died," Harper shot back, realizing too late that she was making a fool of herself thanks to Carl's grating presence. "I'm sorry," she said finally when four sets of eyes turned to her. "Your son is an absolute tool, though, Mrs. Gibbons. I'm surprised you didn't kill him sooner."

Instead of being upset, or calling Harper a filthy liar, Agatha merely croaked out a raspy laugh. "Are you really talking to him?"

"It's more like he's talking to me and he says absolutely nothing of interest."

"That's how he's been his whole life," Agatha conceded. "Give him a message for me, will you?"

"He's here. He can hear anything you say."

"Really?" Agatha brightened considerably. "In that case ... ." She lifted her middle finger and shot it in the air. "I'm not sorry you're dead, Carl. You had it coming. I'm betting we'll end up in the same place so we can sort it all out on the wrong side of the pearly gates. Until then ... suck it."

Harper pressed her lips together to keep from laughing at the surreal situation. Jared sent her an admonishing look, but even he looked tickled by the turn of events. Only Junior seemed unsure.

"Why did you do it, Granny?" he asked, solemn. "Why did you kill him? You had to know that you would get caught."

"I didn't mean to kill him," Agatha offered. "Truly. I didn't mean it. I snuck out of the home that night because I wanted to confront him. Heck, I had a ridiculous notion of being a cat burglar that night, too. I thought I would break into his house, scare him until he gave me what I wanted, or just take something of value and sell it. I didn't think he would be there.

"The thing is, I heard through the grapevine that he was dating Gloria Harlow," she continued, shooting Harper an apologetic look. "I've heard nothing but nice things about you, girlie, but your mother is a known quantity ... and that reputation of hers isn't a good thing."

Harper swallowed hard and nodded. "I'm well aware of my mother's reputation."

"In truth, I thought it was funny when I heard he was dating Gloria. If anyone could chew him up and spit him out, it was her. I always thought what he truly needed was to care about a woman ... and then have her crush him."

"Oh, nice." Carl made a face. "Can you believe this? My role model, ladies and gentlemen."

Harper scowled at him. "Shut up. She's ten times the role model that you were."

Junior watched Harper interact with an invisible version of his father and could do nothing but shake his head. "I see death hasn't changed him."

"Not even a little," Harper agreed.

"How did you do it, Agatha?" Mel asked gently. "Did you take the knife with you?"

She nodded. "Like I said, the plan was steal from him ... or scare him. I didn't want to kill him. He just wouldn't shut up. I didn't know he was going to be there, and when he woke up and found me in his house ... well ... he wouldn't stop saying absolutely ridiculous things. I couldn't deal with it."

Mel nodded in understanding. "Did he tell you he was taking you out of his will?"

"He did," she confirmed. "I didn't even know I was in his will so, at first, I didn't know what to think. He said I was old and didn't need the money anyway. I assumed that meant that Junior was getting that money – all of it – and I was okay with that. Then he told me he was going to spend it on a place in Florida.

"He still planned to allow Junior to inherit," she continued, clearly lost in her story. "He was going to spend the bulk of what he'd squirreled away on a condo in Tampa, though. He didn't even care if there was nothing left to leave Junior."

She turned to Jared, her eyes clear. "I know you probably don't believe this, but that's what sent me over the edge," she said. "I don't know how I raised such a terrible human being. I was angry at myself. I was mostly angry at him, though. I just lashed out ... and once I stabbed him the first time, I couldn't stop."

Harper's stomach gave a small lurch at the visual the older woman was painting.

"Did you think you would get away with it?" Mel asked. "I mean ... did you think no one would look in your direction because you're older?"

Agatha merely shrugged. "I don't know. I don't even know that I wanted to get away with it. I just know that I'm not sorry."

"What about after the fact? Why did you break into the house a second time?"

"To find the will. I wanted to make sure that Junior was getting everything. I didn't care about myself. I still have the will ... and everything is going to him. I just wanted to make sure that Carl didn't do something really bad and cut out Junior. I was going to destroy the will if I found that he'd been playing King Jerk."

Mel let loose a sigh. "You know we're going to have to take you in, right?"

Agatha nodded. "I know."

"Wait." Junior moved to put himself between Mel and his grandmother. "Don't do that. She's elderly. Where is she going to go? Can't you just put her on house arrest?"

"It would be nice if we could," Mel acknowledged. "She's already proven that she can't be trusted to stay here, though. There's no security. She can wander out any time she chooses. I'm sorry. She has to go with us."

Jared rested his hand on Junior's shoulder. "We'll make sure she's comfortable. I'm betting a good attorney – maybe someone you know, like your grandfather – will be able to get her out on a monitor with a little effort."

Junior nodded. "I'll call him."

"That's good. No matter what, she's going to have to spend the night in a cell. The good news is, she'll have the place to herself and we'll make sure she has a nice bunk, plenty of blankets, and takeout from the diner for dinner."

"That's better than the slop they have here," Agatha said brightly. "Maybe jail won't be so bad."

"Maybe," Jared agreed. "We'll sit down with the prosecutor and see what sort of deal can be worked out. There's always a chance you might end up in a hospital – not unlike where you are now – rather than a prison. Given your age ... ."

"Oh, do you hear that?" Agatha playfully smacked Junior's arm. "My age is finally going to be a benefit."

Junior didn't look as if he agreed, but he simply nodded. "Let's get you settled, Granny. I'll grab some of your puzzle books."

"Grab some whiskey, too."

"Don't push it," Mel warned, although he cracked a smile.

Harper slid her eyes to Carl and found him glaring at the scene. "I bet you wish you wouldn't have been such a hateful individual now, don't you?"

"People will remember me forever."

"Not for anything good."

"I'm fine with that."

"I certainly hope so, because it's all you have."

Twenty

Harper was exhausted when she let herself into the house the following Saturday. Jared's truck was in the driveway, which meant he was home, but he'd been burning the candle at both ends over the past few days as he tried to secure a deal for Agatha and she didn't want to risk waking him if he'd finally given in to his weariness and opted to take a nap.

Sure enough, she found him asleep on the couch, a blanket tucked around him and the television muted in the background.

She studied him for a long beat, love washing over her, and then frowned when he cocked an eyebrow and met her gaze.

"I didn't mean to wake you," she said finally, internally cursing herself. "I should've let you sleep."

"I'm fine." He smiled as he stretched. "Besides, there's nothing better than waking up to your face."

Harper snorted. "Someone is feeling charming this afternoon."

"You have no idea." He lifted the blanket and gestured for her to join him. "Come on. I'm tired and all I want is a few minutes with my girl. I think I've earned it."

Because it was true, Harper readily joined him without complaint. "Okay, but just for a few minutes." She slid into his arms, giggling when he offered her a tickle before pulling her close. He let loose a sigh when she pressed her face to his chest and they basked in their shared warmth for a long stretch. Harper was the first to break the silence. "I sent Carl to the other side."

"Good." He kissed her forehead. "I was sick of that jerk hanging around."

"Yes, well, there's no way you were sicker of him than me."

"Try me. The guy was a pervert and wanted to hang around in our bedroom, which meant you became Harper the Prude for those few days. I'm feeling neglected."

"You're not the only one. I had to wait until I could arrange a time for Junior to say goodbye, though. He earned the right."

"He definitely did." Jared pulled back so he could study her eyes. "Was it a warm goodbye?"

"No. Junior tried being calm at the start, but then he unloaded. What's going on with Agatha is weighing on him."

"She's going to be okay," Jared promised, his fingers gentle as he brushed Harper's hair away from her face. "It looks like we're going to plead her down to a manslaughter charge. Technically she'll never be free again, but she won't be in a prison."

"It seems wrong to be thankful for that, doesn't it? I mean ... she is a murderer."

"She is, but if anyone ever pushed people to justifiable homicide, it was Carl. I'm just glad he's moved on. Do you think he went to the good place?"

"I don't know." Harper had been considering that very question herself. "I didn't see a flash this time when I engaged the dream-catcher. It doesn't always happen, so that doesn't necessarily mean anything. I like to think he didn't go to the good place, though. Maybe that makes me petty."

"You're not petty. I'm petty and I'm going to throw a party in our bathtub later because of it."

The picture made Harper smile. "Yes, well ... it's something to look forward to. I am glad that Agatha isn't going to be put into a state prison or anything. The idea of that would haunt me."

"They couldn't have put her in a regular prison anyway. She's too frail because of the stroke. She was always going to a hospital. It became a question of which hospital, but I'm hopeful she'll end up in a local one so Fran and Junior can keep visiting her."

"Junior seemed okay when I saw him today," Harper volunteered. "He's been working with his grandfather on Agatha's defense. He seems happy about the arrangement. He was a little sad while saying goodbye to Carl, but I'm glad I waited to send off that louse. Junior seemed lighter once everything was over and he got the last word. I didn't repeat any of the hateful stuff Carl spouted back, and that only made him more obnoxious."

"I'm glad you waited, too. I'm also glad that he's gone so our romance can continue unabated."

Harper laughed so hard she struggled to suck in a breath. "Who says things like that?"

"I do. I heard it on a Lifetime movie and have been holding it back for just the right moment." He kissed the tip of her nose. "In fact, I'm going to keep saying stuff like that until you let me romance you."

"I have every intention of letting you romance me."

"Good."

"There's just one thing."

Jared waited for her to continue, worry briefly washing over him as he wondered what sort of bad news bomb she was going to drop on him now.

"I had lunch with Zander," she started, choosing her words carefully. "I mentioned to him that you and I were considering taking a vacation."

"Absolutely not." Jared immediately started shaking his head. "He's not going with us. Our last vacation – and I use that term loosely – involved him and mushroom hunting. He didn't stop whining the entire time. I'm not going through that again."

"Hold up." Harper feigned patience as she raised her hand. "That's not what this is about."

Jared arched a suspicious eyebrow. "Oh, you're not about to tell me that Zander invited himself along on our vacation, are you?"

"Nope."

Jared relaxed, if only marginally. He was still expecting bad news. "Then I'm sorry for barking at you. Please continue."

Harper's lips twitched at his adorable expression. "So, the thing is ... Zander had to remind me that we already have a trip planned ... and it's coming up in the next few weeks."

"We do?" Jared drew his eyebrows together. "I'm pretty sure I would remember if we made trip plans."

"Not you and me, but him and me."

Jared frowned. "What? Are you telling me you're going on vacation with Zander instead of me?" He thought he was likely to lose it. "This is like the worst thing to ever happen to me."

"Knock it off." Harper's voice was low and full of warning. "This trip has been planned for two years. I'm the one who forgot about it."

"What trip?"

"It's a cruise. I kind of remembered it when Junior brought up how he wanted to buy a cruise for his mother, but I didn't really think long and hard about it until Zander brought it up. We made plans two years ago because that's how long the waiting list was for this particular getaway."

"So, you and Zander are going on a cruise together. That's just ... great." Jared moved to pull away but she stilled him with a hand on his chest. "What?" His eyes flashed with annoyance.

"The cruise is for paranormal hunters, or people in the business, like us. It's a work cruise and we read about it in a magazine two years ago. I would like to point out that I didn't know you two years ago."

"Whatever." Jared's mood was dour. "Will you let me up?"

"No." She shook her head, firm. "The thing is, we were thinking ahead. We bought four tickets in case we were dating people at the time. Zander was always optimistic about that stuff. Me? Not so much. I agreed to get him off my back, though, because there was no chance we would be able to buy extra tickets, but selling tickets is easy."

Jared stilled. "So ... you have tickets for a cruise and want me to go with you?"

"You and Shawn ... although Zander isn't sure Shawn will be able to go because this is his busiest time of year because everyone makes

New Year's resolutions to lose weight and that means they flood his gym for three months."

To buy himself time, Jared stroked his chin. "What would I be doing on this ship while you're working?"

"Drinking and soaking up sun. The conference only has two scheduled events. It's basically about networking and getting to know people. That's it. You wouldn't be on your own much."

"Well ... ." His expression was hard to read as he met her gaze. "I'm not sure what to say about all this," he admitted after a beat. "It's not exactly the vacation I had in mind."

"I know it's not," she conceded. "I can't pull out, though. I promised. This is a way for everybody to benefit."

"I guess. I want another vacation, though. I want something that's just you and me. I don't care where or when, but I want something that belongs to just the two of us."

"I can make that happen."

"I also want a massage in the tub tonight."

Her lips quirked. "I can make that happen, too."

"Then ... I guess I'm okay with that." He settled back on the couch and considered her serene features. "It might actually be fun."

"It's definitely going to be fun," Harper agreed. "It's only two weeks away. I can't wait ... and if I play my cards right, I'm going to be able to avoid my mother and father all that time so I don't have to listen to their ridiculous excuses for why they've been hiding this sex thing they've been doing."

Jared snickered. "I have a plan to help you avoid them."

"You do? Tell me."

"It involves hiding under the covers and not coming out until we leave."

"I like that idea. Tell me more."

"How about I show you?"

"That's an even better idea."

"I thought you would agree."

She was already tugging her shirt over her head. It was the middle of the afternoon and she didn't even care. "Less talk, more showing."

"Yes, ma'am. Finally something I want to do."